FIVE STAR
TEMPTATION

ESSENCE BESTSELLING AUTHOR

JACQUELIN
THOMAS

HARLEQUIN®

entertain, enrich, inspire™

To the many residents living on Skid Row, underneath the bridges, the alleys and in the parks. My heart is with you; know that your circumstances do not define who you are—you are still that man, woman and child destined for greatness. Do not lose faith.

ISBN-13: 978-0-373-86268-9

FIVE STAR TEMPTATION

Copyright © 2012 by Jacquelin Thomas

Recycling programs for this product may not exist in your area.

For questions and comments about the quality of this book, please contact us at Customer_eCare@Harlequin.ca.

www.Harlequin.com

Printed in U.S.A.

Sage loved the way Ryan's kissable lips parted when he laughed that deep, throaty laugh. He was a very handsome and sexy man—a striking contrast to when she'd met him for the first time.

At the end of the evening, Ryan escorted her up to her place.

Sage unlocked her door, then turned to face Ryan. He leaned over and kissed her. "I really enjoyed our first date."

She resisted the urge to touch the place where his lips had been. Her heart was racing, and Sage could feel her blood rushing through her veins.

She glanced up at Ryan, who said, "I didn't offend you just now, did I?"

"No, you didn't," she answered quickly. Sage's heart fluttered wildly in her chest

His nearness sent a shiver of wanting through her. "Not at all."

Ryan pulled Sage into his arms, his mouth covering hers hungrily.

She returned his kiss with a hunger that belied her outward calm. Burying her face in his neck, Sage breathed a kiss there.

"You have no idea how long I've wanted to kiss you," Ryan confessed.

"Probably as many times as I've wanted you to kiss me."

Books by Jacquelin Thomas

Kimani Romance

The Pastor's Woman
Chocolate Goodies
Teach Me Tonight: Hollington Homecoming
You and I
Case of Desire: Hopewell General
Five Star Attraction
Five Star Temptation

JACQUELIN THOMAS

is an award-winning, bestselling author with more than thirty-five books in print. When she is not writing, she is busy working toward a degree in psychology. Jacquelin and her family live in North Carolina.

Dear Reader,

How many times do we walk past someone who is homeless? How many times do we take a few minutes just to get to know the person? It's one thing to give a few dollars, but Sage Alexander decided to do something more. In the second book of The Alexanders of Beverly Hills series, Sage encounters a man on the street who will forever change her life. Ryan Manning is an investigative reporter who is passionate when it comes to the plight of the homeless. He goes undercover and is surprised not only by Sage Alexander's generous and caring nature, but also by his feelings for her.

This is a cause I have been involved in for years, so it's natural that I would want to write a story about the plight of the homeless. It is my goal to entertain you with a romantic story, but also give you pause for thought the next time you encounter someone down on his/her luck. I hope you will enjoy the ride as you learn more about Ryan and Sage.

May you find it a temptation that is much too hard to resist.

Best regards,

Jacquelin

Chapter 1

"Every woman I know—no matter how successful and ambitious, how financially and emotionally secure— feels panic, occasionally coupled with desperation, if she hits thirty and finds herself unmarried."

Sage Alexander huffed after reading aloud an article by R. G. McCall. "I think *panic* overstates it, let alone *desperation*." She tossed the magazine on the coffee table, nearly knocking over her glass of lemonade.

In a swift move, Sage rescued the glass and took a sip. Still fuming over the article, she uttered, "He's a *man*. What does he really know about women?"

"Perhaps you should finish the article before passing judgment, dear?" her mother suggested with a tiny smile. "Besides, R.G. may be a woman." Barbara Alexander took a long sip of the ice-cold lemonade before setting her glass down on a side table.

Barbara Alexander had decided to spend the day

in Beverly Hills, leaving the peaceful estate home in Pacific Palisades she had come to love. She spent the morning talking to employees and hotel patrons. Sage had prepared a light lunch of grilled chicken salad, yeast rolls and steamed broccoli. They had just finished eating and sat down to relax in the living room while finishing off their glasses of lemonade.

Sage set her glass down, making sure it was secure on the Brazilian-cherry coaster. She wrinkled her nose and shook her head, saying, "Oh, he's definitely a man, Mama. I can tell from the tone of his articles. He comes across as cynical and bitter in his writing as far as I'm concerned. He is someone with a serious chip on his shoulder."

She ran her fingers through her soft curls. "I have no idea why Kellen likes his work so much." Sage made a mental note to ask her brother why he was such a fan of R. G. McCall. "Maybe it's because he's so mysterious. All anyone really knows about him is his name," Sage said.

"I've read a few of his articles," Barbara stated. "I can certainly understand why he is so protective of his identity. He tends to get to the heart of the matter, and a lot of people would prefer to keep the truth buried. I think he's usually unbiased in his articles."

"What he does is throw rocks at you and then hides his hand," Sage sniped. She had no idea why she'd allowed this writer—a man she had never met—to get under her skin like this. Maybe it was because he had chosen a topic that was a bit too close for comfort for Sage.

That topic was her state of singleness.

Barbara chuckled. "Well, he's certainly got you riled up this afternoon. Maybe it's a good thing that you didn't finish reading the article."

Sage gave a grudging nod. "Mama, I'm going to be thirty in October. I really don't need R. G. McCall telling me that I'm in panic mode or desperate just because I would like to settle down and have a family. That man has rubbed me the wrong way this time with his choice in subject."

"Don't take it so personally, dear."

Her mother was right, but it was hard to just ignore the article. It was just one of many on the subject of women reaching the thirty-year mark. It was Sage's birthday wish to find the man of her dreams, although deep down she felt as if her knight in shining armor was nothing more than a dream that would never come true.

Sage had dated a few times since her arrival in Los Angeles, and some of the men were really nice, but they were not the type of man she wanted in her life long-term for various reasons. Sage knew that she had to really be careful in her choices of men due in part to her sudden fame. The Alexander family had been thrust into the limelight, and Sage soon found herself with no shortage of admirers—mostly men who were hoping to land a wealthy heiress.

Her father had inherited the late Robert DePaul's vast estate nearly a year ago, which included the luxury chain of what was now known as the Alexander-DePaul Hotel & Spa. Before the inheritance, they were just a family living a normal life in the small town of Aspen, Georgia, located forty miles west of Atlanta. They were still the same people before the fame and money, but it seemed as though everyone else had changed around them. People close to them treated them differently.

"I don't think there's anything wrong with wanting to be married and ready to start a family before thirty-five," Sage blurted. "I want to be able to enjoy my children before I'm too old."

"You're right, sweetie," Barbara agreed. "There's nothing wrong with the way you feel. As for a family, I wouldn't worry about it. Just trust that the Lord will bring the right man at the right time."

Sage embraced her mother. "Thanks, Mama. I'm so glad I decided to come to Los Angeles. I would have hated being so far away from you." Sage and her brothers Ari, Blaze and Drayden all relocated to Los Angeles to work with their parents at the newly named Alexander-DePaul corporate offices. Her expertise was in real estate, which is why her father had given Sage the responsibility for overall sales of the portfolio of residences located at the hotel in the heart of Beverly Hills and steps from renowned Rodeo Drive.

"I'm glad you're here, too," Barbara responded. "I don't know if Malcolm could handle all this without his children." She rose to her feet. "Thanks so much for lunch and the conversation. I'm supposed to meet your daddy in an hour. I've finally convinced him to give his wardrobe a face-lift."

Sage broke into a grin. "Good luck with that." Her father hated shopping with a passion.

She and Barbara embraced and then headed to the door.

They took the private elevator down to the garage.

"I'll give you a call later in the week," Sage told her

mother. "If you and Daddy don't have any plans, I might drive out to the house this weekend. I want to see the new renovations." Her parents had decided to change some things in the house. They wanted their blended personalities echoed throughout every room.

"We'll be home," Barbara responded.

They embraced again in the parking garage before Barbara headed to her car.

Sage watched her mother get into the car, and she remained glued to the spot until Barbara drove away.

Instead of returning to her penthouse, Sage decided to walk through the hotel. The Beverly Hills property had been inspired by the Spanish Revival architecture and Mediterranean styling that was so prevalent in the area. The interior evoked timeless elegance in sun-drenched colors of gold, salmon, coral and cream, which Sage found awe-inspiring and beautiful.

Her life was perfect, Sage thought to herself.

But it would be even better if she had someone to share it with.

Ryan Manning—aka R. G. McCall—was thirty-two years old, living in New York, and had been working as an investigative reporter for the past ten years with a major newspaper. After his painful divorce and suffering from writer's block, Ryan decided to take a year off. His other love was cooking, so he opened a restaurant in Manhattan. However, his passion for the written word and the truth called him back into news reporting—this time as a freelance writer. His restaurant had turned out to be a very successful venture and was currently managed by his brother.

A news short on television caught Ryan's eye.

The story of Malcolm Alexander inheriting the DePaul estate was still news, even though Robert DePaul had been gone for almost a year. People were still hungry for any information about this family from a small town in Georgia who had captured the hearts of the people in Los Angeles.

What's so special about them? he wondered—outside of being fortunate enough to have Robert DePaul's blood running through their veins.

The late Robert DePaul had been a very generous man during his lifetime. Ryan had heard many stories of Robert paying off medical bills of complete strangers, bestowing cars upon some who could not afford to buy one and even taking in a homeless man, giving him a job. He had often championed the rights of the homeless over the years.

Ryan's current project was going to be a series of articles on the plight of homeless people in large cities—more specifically, Beverly Hills and some of the wealthier areas across the country. He had always been vocal in his criticism of how many of the wealthy residents complain about the homeless, but instead of trying to help, they treat them like criminals. There were those who were eager to spend thousands on a pair of shoes instead of giving a few dollars to a homeless person. To prove his point, Ryan spent some time on the streets of New York gathering firsthand information for his article.

Later that evening, he was flying to Los Angeles. He was going undercover as a homeless man in Beverly Hills. He wanted to profile some of the homeless people who lived in the shadows of Southern California's most affluent areas.

Ryan decided to include the Alexander family in his series along with a select group of celebrities. He wanted to see whether Malcolm Alexander had inherited his father's philanthropic nature. He was curious to see if the Alexander family was as wonderful as everyone assumed. People could only keep up an act for so long.

He knew that the members of the family would eventually slip up, and then the truth would come out about them. Ryan intended to be the one to report it.

To pass the time on the airplane, Ryan decided to draft parts of his article. He hoped that his writing on the subject of homelessness challenged those who were more fortunate to experience what these people had to deal with on a daily basis and moved them to take action.

His hands tapped a steady rhythm on the keyboard of his laptop.

In this manicured community of 35,000, Rolls-Royces and Lamborghinis glide around the city streets of Beverly Hills and movie stars live in grand mansions....

Ryan paused a moment, reading what he had typed, then he added, *However, this city does not just boast of celebrities but is also well-known for its small population of scruffy residents who live in parks, bus shelters and alleys.*

He was not sure that was exactly how he would begin the article, but it worked for the moment.

Ryan leaned his head back and closed his eyes, resting them. He had not realized just how exhausted he was until this very moment. Before leaving New York, he'd had to make sure that his brother had everything under control at the restaurant. Ryan had also wanted to finish another project, so he'd stayed up late last night and woke up early. He closed up the laptop and put it away before falling asleep.

He woke up an hour later. They would not be landing in Los Angeles for another two hours, so Ryan retrieved his laptop and opened it. He decided to attempt to complete the introduction for his article.

The hair on the back of his neck stood up.

Ryan glanced around until he met the gaze of a beautiful young woman. She smiled brightly, pleased that she had caught his attention.

He smiled in return.

Ryan had dated some since his divorce, but his constant traveling prevented him from investing any real time into a relationship. However, Sandra had put him through two years of pure hell. Ryan was pretty sure that he would never marry again.

He refused to allow another woman to shatter his heart into a million pieces ever again.

Chapter 2

Sage and her future sister-in-law, Natasha LeBlanc, exited the Alexander-DePaul Beverly Hills Hotel, heading to a nearby bridal shop on foot.

It was a beautiful and sunny June day, perfect for a stroll. Sage loved the outdoors and often walked to many of the nearby shops and eateries.

"I love seeing Ari with Joshua," Sage commented as they walked. "I'm so glad that he has you both in his life."

Natasha smiled. "He's not my son's biological father, but I couldn't ask for anyone more wonderful than Ari."

Her oldest brother had married his childhood sweetheart right out of college, but lost her to cancer a couple years ago. She had worried that Ari would never stop grieving for April. Then Natasha and her son, Joshua, entered his life a year ago, giving Ari a reason for living again.

"But after tomorrow, it will be official," Natasha stated. "I'm relieved that the adoption has gone through without a hitch. Although I have to confess that there is this tiny part of me that resents the fact that my ex-husband wants nothing to do with his son." She released a short sigh. "No need to worry about the past, though. I have Ari."

"If you say he completes you, I'm going to barf," Sage interjected with a small chuckle.

Natasha laughed.

Out of the corner of her eye, Sage noticed a lone homeless man standing near the entrance.

Her steps slowed as their eyes met and held.

The trance was broken when two hotel security members walked outside, gesturing for him to leave the property grounds.

Sage quickly intervened. "He's not doing anything."

One of the men told her, "Some of the guests have complained, Miss Alexander—"

"I understand that you're doing your job, Tom," she responded. "But everything is fine. You can go back inside now."

Sage told Natasha, "Wait here a moment, please." She walked over to the stranger in clothes that had seen better days and said, "I'm sorry for the actions of my security personnel." She pulled a hundred-dollar bill out of her wallet and offered it to the homeless man. "I hope this will help you in some way."

He was clearly surprised by her generosity. "Thank you. I appreciate your kindness."

Sage noted the rich timbre of his baritone voice.

"If you're hungry, I can arrange a meal for you," Sage said.

He held up the money and responded, "This is more than enough."

He thanked her again before walking away.

Sage watched him for a moment as he headed in the other direction. "I feel so bad for him," she said in a low voice.

"That was really nice of you," Natasha murmured.

"He definitely needs it more than I do," Sage responded as they continued on to the bridal shop.

Although she considered him a fleeting thought, Sage found she could not force him out of her mind. It was as if some invisible thread drew her to him. It was not something she could fully explain because she did not understand it herself.

This unknown stranger who had fallen on hard times had left an indelible impression on her.

Ryan stared down at the hundred-dollar bill in his hand in disbelief.

The daughter of Malcolm Alexander had given him the money without any hesitation. It was almost as if she had been expecting him.

He had seen enough pictures of her to recognize Sage Alexander. However, none of the photos truly did her justice.

She was gorgeous.

He had the pleasure of meeting Robert DePaul a few years ago at a political fundraiser. Ryan found that she possessed those same steel-gray eyes as her father and Robert, her grandfather. She was tall and slender, with curves in all the right places. She wore her long dark brown hair in its natural curly state.

Ryan's eyes stayed on Sage as she and her friend strolled down the sidewalk and across the street to a bridal shop. He couldn't help but wonder if she was always this generous or if this had just been some random act of kindness.

He heard the whine of a baby and glanced over his shoulder.

A young woman who looked to be in her early twenties was trying to soothe a tiny infant swaddled tightly in a blanket. She held the baby close to her heart and appeared to be whispering to the child.

She reached into the shopping cart, fumbled through a few bags and then frowned. Whatever she was looking for was long gone. She kissed the top of her baby's head and continued to try and comfort the infant. Her blue eyes were dull and pained and her blond hair looked as if it could use a good washing.

Without a second thought, Ryan strode over to her.

"Miss, can I help you with anything?"

She silently surveyed him from head to toe before shaking her head. "I'm fine."

"The baby—"

"She needs to be changed," the young woman murmured.

Ryan glanced down into the shopping cart. She didn't possess much, but there was no sign of diapers—cloth or otherwise.

"This woman just walked out of the hotel and gave me this money, but I want you to have it. Looks like you may need to purchase diapers."

Her eyes widened in surprise when she saw the hundred-dollar bill in his hand.

"I can't take this from you," she whispered, tears in her eyes. Her gaze traveled slowly over his attire. "You need it as much as I do."

"I'll be okay," Ryan assured her. "I want you to have it. Use it for the baby." He could tell that the infant was only a few weeks old. "She's beautiful."

After a short deliberation, she accepted the money and smiled. "God bless you for your kindness. Thank you so much."

"When was the last time you had a hot meal?" Ryan asked.

"A few days now," she responded. "My milk is drying up, so I think I'm going to have to get formula."

"Hey, I'm about to get something to eat. Why don't you and your beautiful little daughter join me? We can stop somewhere and get the diapers so you can change her first."

He saw the hesitation in her eyes. "I'm sorry. I didn't mean to scare you. My name is Ryan, and I have nothing but honorable intentions."

"I'm Paige, and this is Cassie. Ryan, you've done so much already. We really don't want to take advantage of your kindness."

"You wouldn't be," he said. "Paige, it looks like you need a friend. I assure you that I am not looking for anything in return."

They walked until they found a corner store and bought diapers, a set of bottles, formula and some onesies for the baby.

Ryan pointed to the restaurant across the street. "We can eat there."

Together, they crossed the street.

"I'll wait out here," Paige said, looking uncomfortable. "I need to change Cassie anyway. Besides, I'm pretty sure they don't want us to come inside."

Just as he was about to enter the restaurant, a young man dressed like one of the waitstaff met him at the door.

"I can take your order," he said, "if you have money to pay."

Ryan had forgotten he was dressed like a homeless person. It was clear that the waiter feared they would offend the other patrons. He stepped away from the door. "I wouldn't be here if I didn't have money," he retorted. "I want to order two burgers, fries and drinks to go."

"You sure you have enough money to pay for all this?" the young man asked.

"Like I said, I wouldn't have ordered it if I didn't," Ryan responded, angered by the look of disdain on the waiter's face. He pulled out two twenty-dollar bills. *"Keep the change."*

Embarrassed, the waiter muttered, "I'll place your order right now. It'll be about ten minutes."

Ryan strolled over to one of the outdoor tables where Paige sat playing with her baby girl.

"Why are you out here on the streets, Ryan?" Paige asked. "You obviously have money."

"The only reason I have this money is because some rich woman gave it to me when I was standing outside the Alexander-DePaul Hotel," he responded honestly.

"Then I saw you, and I wanted to help. A young mother and her baby should not be on the streets."

The waiter appeared with two tall glasses of ice water and two sodas. He set them down on the table and left as discreetly as he had arrived. He returned a few minutes later with their food.

"Where are you from?" Ryan inquired. He could hear a hint of a Southern accent in her voice.

"I'm from Atlanta, Georgia," Paige responded. "I came to Los Angeles to be with my boyfriend. He plays the sax, and he's trying to get into the music business. Things were good between us until I got pregnant. Then we started to argue and fight all the time. After Cassie was born, I thought we were getting back on track, but two weeks ago, he left to buy diapers and never returned. I couldn't pay the rent for the hotel we were staying in, so I had to leave."

Ryan felt a surge of anger rise in him as he listened to Paige's story. What man could just walk away from his child like that?

It was obvious that this man never really cared for Paige. Ryan was careful not to voice his opinion aloud. He did not want to say anything that would add to the young woman's pain.

"Have you decided on your color scheme yet?" Sage inquired.

"I was actually thinking about a mint-green and vintage-purple theme," Natasha said. "They are two of my favorite colors." She paused a moment before adding, "Oh, and I've found what I think is the perfect bridesmaid dress. It's by Alvina Valenta. She is an extraordinary designer, and her dresses are known for their details and elegance."

"I'm just glad that you didn't choose soft pastel colors," Sage announced as they entered the bridal shop. "They do absolutely nothing for my complexion. You know weddings are all about the bridesmaids, don't you?"

Laughing, Natasha walked up to the counter to check in for their appointment.

While they waited, Sage's gaze traveled the length of the shop, eyeing the vast number of wedding gowns, bridesmaid dresses and other formal wear. She couldn't wait for the day when it would be her turn to get married.

Her dream wedding wasn't filled with lots of glitz, glamour and hundreds of wedding guests. Instead, she wanted a more intimate and romantic ceremony—perhaps a destination wedding.

"What do you think about this one?" Natasha asked, drawing Sage out of her reverie.

She surveyed the gown in her future sister-in-law's hand. "It's pretty, but I don't think it looks like you."

"Really?"

Sage nodded. "I don't know why, but I just can't really see you in this dress. Maybe it's because there's so much lace. You don't strike me as the ribbons, ruffles or bows type of girl."

"You're right," Natasha agreed. "I prefer more simple lines but thought I'd do something different for my wedding."

"No," Sage interjected. "Your gown should definitely echo your personality." She walked over to a nearby rack and selected a dress. "Now, I think that this one looks like you, Natasha."

"Oh, my…" Natasha murmured as she fingered the soft, delicate chiffon. "This is stunning."

Sage agreed. "You should try it on."

Anna, the bridal consultant standing nearby, walked over to them. "I'll take this to the dressing room."

"Ari told me that I could have my dress designed, but I think I'd rather buy one off the rack." Natasha pressed the dress against her body. "I really love this one."

"Try it on," Sage encouraged.

She strolled around the store, pausing every now and then to look at a gown. Sage already knew how she wanted her dress to look. While Natasha wasn't interested in having a one-of-a-kind wedding gown, Sage felt otherwise.

Natasha walked out of the dressing room with the assistance of Anna. She looked like a vision from heaven in the eggshell-tinted strapless gown made of Tomen chiffon and lace embellished with Swarovski crystals and a sweetheart neckline. The unbelievable draping across Natasha's torso completed the elegant vision.

"So what do you think?" Natasha prompted.

"You look beautiful," Sage murmured. "I think this is the one for you."

"Ms. LeBlanc, you look exquisite," Anne complimented. "From everything you've told me, I agree with Ms. Alexander. This is the wedding dress for you."

Natasha continued to gaze at her reflection.

"I'm loving it," Sage said. "I can't wait for my brother to see you in this gown."

"I love it, too," Natasha responded. "This is the dress

for me. My search is over for the perfect wedding gown."
She glanced over at Anna and said, "Would you bring
out the dress I selected for the bridesmaids, please? I
want Sage's opinion on the choice."

Anna walked into a back room and returned a few
minutes later, carrying a stunning knee-length satin
sheath in a purple/platinum duet.

Sage fell in love with the draped strapless sweetheart
neckline with natural waist and draped skirt. "Natasha,
it's gorgeous. I *love* it."

"I thought that you would," she responded. "It's going
to look great on you, Zaire and my sister."

Sage held the dress up to her and eyed her reflection
in the mirror. "This is a beautiful dress. I especially
like that it's one I can wear again. I have a closet full
of bridesmaid gowns that were only for that one day."

"I'll set up a dressing room for you," Anna stated.
"While you change, I'll have the seamstress come out
to perform the fitting for Ms. LeBlanc."

Sage hummed softly as she strolled into a nearby
dressing room to try it on. She couldn't wait to see how
the dress looked on her body.

"You look beautiful," Natasha said when Sage walked
out. "You need very few alterations. It nearly fits you
perfectly."

Sage agreed. "Natasha, I really love this dress. This
dress is so *me*."

"How do you think Zaire will feel about it?"

"Natasha, she's going to love it, as well," Sage assured her. "My sister and I have similar taste when it
comes to clothes. We're also the same size, so you don't
have to worry about having her dress altered. Besides,

she's planning to come out here in a couple of weeks. Zaire says that school has been hectic for her and she needs a little break. I know that grad school is intense, but I think my little sister is missing the family. She can't just leave Atlanta and be home in an hour anymore."

"My sister and I are the same way."

"I'm looking forward to meeting your family, especially Natalie," Sage stated. "It sounds like she and I have a lot in common."

"You do," Natasha responded.

Sage waited patiently while the seamstress worked with Natasha to make sure the gown fit her body perfectly for her big day. Every now and then, her eyes would travel around the shop, gazing at row after row of wedding gowns. *My time will come,* she silently assured herself.

When Sage returned to the hotel, she glanced around before walking through the entrance.

I wonder what happened to that homeless man, she thought. Maybe he was somewhere having a hot meal; at least she hoped he had spent some of the money she had given him on a good meal. He didn't resemble a drug addict or alcoholic.

She shook her head in confusion.

It was strange, but Sage felt as if their souls were connected. The feeling was so strong that she knew deep down that she had not seen the last of this man who had left such a strong impression on her.

Sage made her way up to her penthouse, humming softly. She was looking forward to relaxing in a hot bath.

An image of the homeless man flittered through her

mind, and Sage suddenly felt guilty. She felt blessed beyond measure, but she also knew about the thousands of people who lived on the streets all over the country. Many of them had given up on hope for a better future.

Sage knew that she could not save the world, but she wanted to find a way to help the people she could. One person at a time.

Chapter 3

"How long have you been living on the streets?" Ryan asked before biting into his hamburger. He chewed slowly, savoring the combination of lettuce, tomato and grilled onions. After living on the streets of New York, he had a renewed appreciation for something as simple as a hamburger.

"Just a few days off and on since my boyfriend left," Paige answered before wiping her mouth on the edge of the paper napkin. "I was able to stay at the shelter for four nights, but last night they didn't have any more beds. I've been trying to find a job, but I don't have a babysitter, so I have to take Cassie with me."

"Have you considered moving back home?" Ryan questioned.

Paige nodded. "I could do that, but it's not what I want. My mama has enough to take care of, and she don't need me and Cassie adding to her burden. She raised six kids all by herself, and now she is raising three of my nieces. All I need is a job, and I can take it from there. I'm not afraid of hard work."

"What type of work are you looking for?" Ryan inquired.

"Anything," Paige responded. "I have general office skills and only two years of college, but I'll clean houses or hotels, babysit—anything outside of breaking the law."

Ryan smiled. "I'm glad to hear that. I don't think I have enough money to bail you out of jail."

She laughed. "Ryan, I really appreciate all you've done for me."

"I'm glad I could help."

Paige bit into her burger. "This is so delicious. I don't remember the last time I had a hamburger." She shook her head sadly. "I just wish that I could find a job. I'd work two jobs if it would help me get a place to live and take care of my baby."

Ryan wiped his mouth. "Paige, I'm going to pay for you and Cassie to stay in a hotel for a month. Hopefully, this will give you some time to find work and a babysitter."

She gasped in surprise and leaned forward, saying, "That lady must have given you a lot of money. Ryan, I can't have you doing this for me. You should be spending this money on yourself."

He shook his head no. "I don't have a new baby, Paige."

She teared up once more. "Ryan, you don't even know me. Why are you being so kind?"

"This woman I ran into earlier knows nothing about

me, yet she was kind enough to care and try to make my life a little more comfortable. I'm just paying it forward."

"We can share the hotel room as friends," Paige suggested. "You can get one with two beds."

Ryan was touched by her sensitivity. "I'll be just fine, Paige. You don't have to worry about me."

"You really don't have to do this, Ryan. I'll manage somehow."

He shook his head. "It's all settled, Paige. You and Cassie will stay at the hotel. I feel confident that you are going to find a job soon. I'll watch the baby for you when you have interviews if you need me to."

"How do I reach you?" she asked. "Don't tell me that this woman gave you a cell phone, too."

Ryan chuckled. "I'll come by and check with you every day."

"Why won't you just stay at the hotel with me? Wouldn't that be easier? Actually, I think I'd feel safer if you were there," Paige confessed. "Cassie's a pretty good baby, too. She only wakes up once a night usually."

"Maybe just a couple of nights," he responded after a moment.

They left the restaurant and walked to the bus stop. Ryan removed Paige's contents from the shopping cart and carried the meager possessions.

Although he secretly preferred to set them up in a much nicer hotel, Ryan had to settle for a motel. He was undercover and had to remain so until all of his research was complete. Ryan would not risk placing his work in jeopardy by sharing his real identity with Paige. He had probably done too much for her already, but he couldn't just leave a young mother and her child out on the streets.

While the baby slept, Paige went into the bathroom to take a shower. Ryan used this time to quickly jot down notes of his time with Paige and how she ended up on the streets. She was defenseless with a newborn, and he feared that if he didn't do everything in his power to help her, Paige would become a prostitute—willingly or unwillingly. Worse, she could become hooked on drugs, and there's no telling how the baby would fare in either situation.

After her bath, Sage slipped on a pair of denim shorts and a T-shirt. She sat down on the plush sofa in her living room and removed her sandals. She stretched out her full length on the piece of furniture and closed her eyes. She thought again about the homeless man who had been standing outside the hotel.

Sage hoped that the money would enable him to enjoy a good meal and maybe even a clean shirt or two. She prayed that he would not use the money for drugs, although he did not seem like a drug abuser.

She drifted off to sleep.

It was almost six when she awakened forty-five minutes later.

Sage had to get ready for a fundraising event. She and her mother were attending the auction benefiting breast cancer. Thankfully, it was being held here at the hotel, so Sage didn't have to worry about traffic or arriving late. She still hadn't gotten used to traveling along the congested Los Angeles freeways.

She rose to her feet and walked barefoot across the hardwood floors to her bedroom.

Sage dressed in a one-shoulder Grecian-style gown in a teal-blue color with shimmering gold highlights. She ran her fingers through soft waves, fluffing her hair to give it a fuller look.

Sage checked the clock on her nightstand. She had to meet her mother downstairs in less than fifteen minutes.

While waiting for Barbara to arrive, Sage spent a few minutes in one of the boutiques, surveying a newly arrived collection of jewelry.

"You have never been one much for jewelry," a voice said behind her.

Sage turned around to face Drayden. "They have some beautiful pieces in this collection, but as you said, I'm not much for jewelry." She glanced down at her ringless fingers. "The only ring I'll ever wear is a wedding ring." She took note of his tuxedo and asked, "Where are you going?"

"Mom rangled me and Blaze into attending this fundraiser, too," Drayden replied. "Ari and Natasha are also attending. If Dad wasn't flying out to San Francisco tonight, I'm sure he'd be here with us."

Sage gave him a knowing smile. "Fundraisers are a family event, according to Mama."

Shortly after the rest of her family arrived, they headed toward the ballroom. Sage pretended to be attentive, but her mind was preoccupied. She was still thinking about the homeless man. She was curious about him.

She had seen enough homeless people on the streets and in the shelters to recognize that there was something different about him. He did not wear that same look of hopelessness, that yearning-to-be-whole-again vibe that hung on their bodies like a blanket. His downward spiral was something that he had suffered recently.

"What are you thinking about?" Blaze leaned over and whispered in her ear. "You look a million miles away."

"I was thinking about this person I saw earlier today. He was homeless."

Blaze met her gaze. "You gave him money, didn't you?"

She nodded. "I know how you feel about that, but I have good instincts about people, and this guy is no drug addict or alcoholic."

"But he could be gambling," Blaze suggested. "There is a reason he is on the streets, sis."

"Or he could have lost his job and his home," Sage countered. "Blaze, not everyone who is homeless is on the streets because of vices. Sometimes it is just plain bad luck."

"I agree," Blaze stated, "but they are the minority."

"You should come to the shelter with me next weekend." Sage took a sip of her ice water. "Once you meet some of these people, I think your opinion will change greatly."

"I'll think about it," he responded. Blaze rose to his feet and held out his hand. "C'mon, let's go show these people how we used to get down in Georgia."

Sage chuckled. "I'll sit this one out. You go ahead. I'm sure you won't have a problem finding a dance partner."

Shortly after eleven, Barbara confessed she was tired and ready to leave.

Both of her brothers couldn't have been more relieved

by their mother's decision. Sage picked up her purse, and they left as they had arrived—as a family.

Blaze joined Sage in her residence when they left the fundraiser.

"So, how do you like living in Beverly Hills?" she asked her brother after they settled down in the living room. "Do you ever regret moving out here?" Sage removed her designer high heels; they were cute but uncomfortable.

"Why do you ask?"

"Sometimes you look really sad, Blaze." Sage shrugged. "Ever since you came back from Las Vegas last year, you haven't really seemed yourself." She paused a moment before asking, "Blaze, did something happen while you were there?"

His expression was instantly guarded. "Like what?"

"Did you meet someone?" Sage inquired.

Blaze waited a moment before responding, as if searching for the right words. "I met someone, but it didn't last long. I guess it was over before it really started."

"It seems like you really cared for her, especially if you are still haunted by her. Do you want to talk about it?"

He shook his head no. "There's really nothing to talk about, sis."

Sage didn't press her brother. She knew Blaze well enough to know that he would open up whenever he was ready. Until then, it was best to drop the subject.

"How about you?" Blaze asked. "How's your love life going?"

She broke into laughter. "What love life? I don't know what that is."

"Have you found it harder to meet someone since our lives have changed?"

Sage nodded. "I don't trust as easily as I did in the past. I guess it's because I have to wonder if it's me or our father's money that guys want." Sighing softly, she leaned back against the cushions. "I'm happy for Daddy and I love my job and even living here in Beverly Hills, but I hate being the focus of the media, dealing with cousin Harold and his drama and wondering if people like us for ourselves."

Blaze nodded in agreement. "Some of the women I've gone out with once or twice expect me to take them shopping or pay their bills. It's *crazy*. It's just dinner and a movie. I'm not trying to marry them."

"I want a man who wants me for me and not for what our parents have. He inherited Robert DePaul's money—not us."

"We are his heirs, though," Blaze interjected. "Sage, you might as well get used to the reality that we will never be able to escape the DePaul legacy."

Ryan made sure that Paige had everything she needed before leaving her and the baby at a small motel on Sunset Boulevard.

He promised to check up on her later in the day. She was a nice young woman who needed a break in life. He was going to make sure that she received one, too.

Ryan was on his way back to the Alexander-DePaul Hotel in Beverly Hills. He was hoping to see the beautiful heiress who had locked eyes with him and given him money without so much as a second thought. A few people passing by tossed a dollar or two his way, but Sage Alexander had been the only one who dared to look him in the eye. She never once averted her gaze— a quality Ryan liked in people. His first impression of her was a good one.

Sage's unselfish gesture had given him a great intro for his article. Her family was one of the main subjects in the article, and it pleased Ryan that Sage appeared to be as generous a benefactor as her grandfather.

There was much more he wanted to learn about Sage and her family.

Sage Alexander.

Her beauty mesmerized him. She was an unforgettable woman, and Ryan found himself wanting to know more about her on both a professional *and* personal level.

Giving him a hundred dollars was one thing but actually holding a conversation with a homeless man was another story. Ryan didn't want to frighten Sage in any way, so he had to be careful in his approach.

He had been careful not to settle too close to the hotel property upon his arrival. Ryan did not want to risk police involvement or getting arrested. No one knew the real identity of R. G. McCall outside of his editors, and Ryan wanted to keep it this way.

Ryan wanted to stay as anonymous as possible.

Chapter 4

A black Mercedes pulled up and parked in front of the hotel doors.

Ryan watched as Drayden Alexander stepped out of the driver's seat and walked around the car, handing the keys to the valet. He was dressed in a suit that fit nicely but was off the rack. Ryan wasn't much for custom-tailored suits either.

Drayden never once glanced in Ryan's direction; instead, he seemed focused and walked with purpose.

Ryan noted Drayden made a point to greet everyone by name, although he didn't break his stride.

He saw security walking toward the entrance and quickly moved away from the side of the building. Ryan kept walking until he reached the end of the property.

"Get a job, you bum," someone yelled out of a passing car.

He shook his head sadly. Some people could be so

ignorant at times. Most people were not homeless by choice or because they didn't want to work. For most, it was an aftershock of the earthquake in their lives that had attempted to destroy them. Rebuilding lives after an earthquake took time, and often victims needed help financially and emotionally.

A man pushing a shopping cart paused and asked, "You find any good eats 'round here?"

Ryan shook his head. "Not yet. I heard that the restaurant on the corner will give you a hot meal."

The man snorted and then moved on.

Ryan resisted the urge to try and hold a conversation with the man, because he wanted to see Sage again. He didn't know why or how, but a connection had been made and Ryan always followed his instincts.

Sage showed off a vacant residence to a couple of prospective buyers. "The bedrooms are all spacious," she told them. "There are a limited number of residences ranging from two to five bedrooms with ample square footage to accommodate housekeepers, personal assistants or nannies."

"Is there a private garage for residents?" the husband inquired. "And is it a two-car garage?"

"Each residence comes with a two-car garage," Sage responded. "The residents have a personal valet. You can just drop your keys with the valet and take the private elevator up to the penthouse floors."

She allowed them some privacy as they walked through the residence. Sage could tell that they were already falling in love with the place. She expected to write a contract before they left her office. The Broadway producer and his wife were here in town for a promotional tour and decided to check out some properties for a Los Angeles–based home.

She called Ari as soon as the couple left an hour later.

"Guess what I have in my hand…?"

"I have no idea," Ari replied. "What is it?"

"I just sold unit 802," she announced.

"Really? That's wonderful," he told Sage. "That's the one like Mom and Dad's, right?"

"Yes," she confirmed. "And they didn't even haggle over the asking price. The wife was the one who really loved the unit. I should probably give her a commission because she was the one who really sold her husband on the place. I think he would've preferred something near the beach."

"I'm sure you helped in that respect," Ari responded. "You have always been one who could talk sugar out of candy."

She laughed. "I don't know about that, but I am going to get off this phone and treat myself to a nice lunch to celebrate."

"If you can hold off for about an hour, I'll join you," Ari told her.

"Rain check," Sage said in response to his offer. "I'm starving, but just remember that you owe me lunch."

"Hey, when was it the plan for me to pay for lunch?"

"When you considered joining me," Sage responded with a chuckle. "Love you much, big brother."

"I love you, too."

They ended the call.

Sage grabbed her keys and purse from the sofa table. She strolled across the gleaming wood floors, her heels tapping in rhythm with her stride. She smiled as she considered her recent sale and the commission.

"Yes," she whispered while waiting for the private elevator car.

Franklin walked out of the unit that belonged to Ari. "Good afternoon, Ms. Alexander."

"I'm never going to get you to just call me Sage, am I?"

He smiled. "It is a title of honor. You should wear it proudly."

"But you're family, Franklin," she countered, "not just another employee."

Touched by her words, he gave a slight nod. "You are too kind, Ms....Sage."

"I mean every word, Franklin. You and your daughter are now a part of our family. We love you both."

The elevator arrived, and they both stepped inside.

"Franklin, are we still donating food to the homeless shelters?" Sage inquired.

"I believe so, but I can check to make sure."

"No, I'll do it," she said. "I know that we are in need of a new manager for the restaurant, so I don't want the donation falling through the cracks."

Sage paused briefly to continue her conversation with Franklin and then made her way to the lobby area.

She was surprised to see her parents. "Hey, what are y'all doing here?" Sage inquired.

Barbara embraced her daughter. "We're meeting Natasha and Ari here for lunch to discuss plans for the wedding. You should join us."

"Ari isn't going to be here any time soon. I'm not sure he even remembered that he was having lunch with you all," Sage interjected. "I can't wait that long because I'm starved."

"He didn't until I called, so we're not waiting on your brother," her father said. "I didn't eat breakfast."

Sage followed them to the hotel restaurant where they were seated immediately. She sat down beside her mother. "I have something to tell you both."

"What is it, sweetie?" Malcolm asked.

"I have a contract on my desk for unit 802."

Barbara grinned. "Congratulations, dear."

Malcolm nodded in approval. "Can't say I'm surprised."

A man seated at the table across from them opened a newspaper.

"I certainly hope he's not reading anything that R. G. McCall has to say," she said in a low voice.

"Sage, are you still bothered by that article you read in that magazine?" Barbara asked.

"What article?" Malcolm inquired.

"It's nothing really, Daddy," Sage responded. "Some guy with a chip on his shoulder wrote that a woman turning thirty is so desperate to have a man in her life that she will marry the first one to look her way."

Her father laughed.

Wearing a frown, Sage inquired, "What's so funny?"

"Well, you have been bemoaning your state of singleness lately."

"I wouldn't say that I was desperate," she replied curtly. "Besides, there's nothing wrong with me wanting to get married and raise a family."

"This is true," Malcolm stated. "Your mother and I

want that for you, as well. Perhaps we should post some type of bonus or something."

Sage's mouth dropped open in surprise. "If a man has to be paid to marry me then I don't want him."

Barbara laughed. "Stop teasing your daughter."

Sage folded her arms across her chest. "That's really not funny, Daddy."

Malcolm reached over and took Sage's hand, giving it a loving squeeze. "I'm sorry, sweetie. I didn't mean to upset you."

"I know you didn't, but you're right," she admitted. "My singleness is beginning to bother me. I can't deny that I want a husband and a family, but I'm not desperate or anything. I'm just ready for marriage. I'm tired of dating and the relationship goes nowhere."

"I have a feeling that you are going to meet the man of your dreams soon," Barbara told her.

Sage smiled. "Mama, you were always a romantic."

She picked up her menu, scanning the entrées. "I'm in the mood for seafood today."

"So am I," Malcolm responded. "I think I'm going to have the grilled tilapia."

"That sounds delicious," Sage murmured. "Mama, what are you ordering?"

"I think I'll have the grilled chicken and ravioli."

"I'm going to order the tilapia," Sage decided aloud. She glanced toward the restaurant entrance and said, "It's about time those two showed up."

Ari and Natasha made their way over to the table and sat down.

"Hey," Ari greeted. "Sorry we're late. Natasha's meeting ran longer than we expected."

Natasha nodded in agreement. "It's my fault."

"We haven't ordered yet," Malcolm stated, "so you're just in time."

The waiter arrived a few minutes later to take their orders.

"So where are you two with the wedding plans?" Barbara inquired after he walked away from their table. "Have you narrowed down where you want to have the wedding ceremony?"

Natasha smiled and nodded. "We'd like to have the wedding at the house. Ari and I feel this is the perfect place to begin our life together as husband and wife."

Barbara gave a slight nod of approval. "I think it's a wonderful idea."

Sage agreed. She was absolutely thrilled for Ari, but there was a part of this that highlighted the fact that there was no man present in her life. It wasn't the lack of male companionship literally, because she was constantly approached by celebrities, business professionals, athletes and even a couple of college students.

However, Sage was very selective and cautious when it came to relationships because of a bad experience she went through in college—something that still haunted her from time to time. She was determined that no other man would ever deceive her again.

Sage thought about the homeless man from the day before. She had not been able to forget about him. It was the expression that was on his face—the one that said although his circumstances looked as if he was past hope, he was still optimistic about life.

Impulsively, Sage headed toward the lobby exit. She

walked outside, her eyes surveying the surroundings. A way of relief swept through Sage upon seeing him.

What am I doing?

She didn't wait for the answer. Instead, Sage inhaled deeply and then exhaled slowly before approaching him.

"I thought you might be out here," she said. "My name is Sage. What's yours?"

"Ryan," he responded. "Ryan Manning."

"I hope that you were able to enjoy a hot meal and a clean bed. I know that the shelters are overflowing, and they can't accommodate everyone."

"Yes. Thank you for the money. I can't tell you how much it helped."

She smiled. "I'm glad I could help you in some small way." Sage paused a moment before continuing. "Actually, I would like to try and really help you, Ryan. I can't explain it, but my gut instinct tells me it's something I should do."

Ryan's eyes widened in surprise, but he remained silent.

Sage was well aware of the curious glances and stares she was receiving from people all around them, including the hotel employees, but she didn't care. She had to do what was in her heart.

"I hope I won't offend or embarrass you by this question, but when was the last time you had a bath and some clean clothes?"

He gave a slight shrug. "It's been a few days."

"Well, we're going to change that right now," Sage stated. "I want you to come with me."

She couldn't remember the last time she had acted

so impulsively, but it was too late to turn back now. Sage had always trusted her instincts; this time would be no different.

Chapter 5

Hotel security hurried toward them, but Sage quickly waved them away. "He is with me," she told them. "There's nothing to worry about. I'm fine."

Ryan silently noted that the two men backed off immediately, although their body language signaled that they were still on alert and ready to pounce, if needed.

He was still in shock that Sage had not only given him money but was now leading him into the Alexander-DePaul Beverly Hills Hotel.

Patrons gasped and stared in horror as they made their way through the lobby. However, Sage Alexander appeared to be oblivious to the stir she was causing. She walked over to the front desk. She was speaking so softly that Ryan had no idea what she was saying to the reservation manager.

He dropped his head to keep from meeting the gazes of anyone.

"I'm going to take you to a room on the second level," Sage told him. "You can shower and shave, and I'll have Franklin bring you some clean clothes."

"Franklin?"

"He's the head of our security and someone I trust with my life."

"I appreciate all you're trying to do for me, but Ms.… you don't know a thing about me. For all you know, I could be a serial killer."

"That's why I want Franklin to meet you," Sage responded. "He'll let me know if there is anything I need to worry about where you're concerned."

Ryan chuckled. "Do I need to worry about a cavity search?"

Laughing, Sage shook her head no.

"Ms.—"

"It's Alexander, but please…just call me Sage," she interjected quickly.

"Okay, Sage…why are you doing all this for me? Are you some type of Good Samaritan?"

"I wouldn't say that," she responded with a smile. "I just care about people, that's all."

A young woman with blond hair and wearing a trendy-looking business suit greeted Sage but took one look at Ryan and then glanced away.

"I apologize for her rudeness," Sage stated as they walked to the elevators.

"People are uncomfortable when staring poverty in the face," Ryan responded. "They know that it exists, but they do not want to put a face to it."

Ryan had been a guest at the hotel in the past. In fact, it was one of his favorite places to stay when in

Los Angeles. He was acutely aware that everyone was staring at him—some with open disdain. He cleared his throat softly.

"Really, why are you doing all this?" he asked when they were alone in the elevator.

Ryan reminded himself that he had to tread carefully with Sage and not ask too many questions. He didn't want to make her suspicious.

"You obviously need help, and I am in a position to help you," Sage responded truthfully. "I would want someone to lend a helping hand if I needed one."

"So you just go around picking up homeless people?"

"No, I don't," Sage stated. "I'm good at reading people and…well, when I saw you yesterday I felt in my gut that I had to do something to help you."

"I don't mean to sound ungrateful," he told her.

"It's okay," Sage responded. "You don't know me either, so I can understand why you would be apprehensive." She awarded him a bright smile. "All I can say is that it was placed on my heart to bless you."

Ryan followed her off the elevator. Sage had a little bounce to her walk; her hips swayed gently from side to side. She was dressed in a pair of navy slacks and a bright orange and navy silk top. Her long hair was neatly secured in a ponytail by an orange-and-navy barrette.

She was a woman with a mission, and Ryan could tell from her demeanor that she would let no one thwart that determination.

Ryan considered all of the women he had come across throughout his life and could truly say that he had never met a woman like her. His ex-wife was also a very determined woman, only she had no problem using lies or

manipulation to get whatever she wanted. It never occurred to her that perhaps being honest was the way to
go, especially if one wanted to earn trust.

Inside of the luxury hotel suite, Sage handed Ryan
a menu. "Feel free to order whatever you want to eat.
It's my treat."

He hadn't been aware that he was staring at her until
she said, "What is it? Why are you looking at me like
that?"

Ryan cleared his throat. "I'm sorry. I…I just can't
get over how generous you are. I've never met anyone
like you."

"I'm just me," Sage responded with a shrug. "There's
nothing special about a person who cares about others.
I'm one of many."

"I don't agree," he responded. "To some degree, that
quality makes you rare. People *say* they care, but I believe that actions speak a lot louder than words."

"I knew there was something very different about
you," Sage murmured.

"What do you mean?" Ryan asked, instantly on
guard.

"Just that I've been around many of the homeless. I
volunteer at one of the shelters twice a month. I know
that you're educated. There's actually many layers to
you."

"Not all homeless people have some sort of impair-
ment," Ryan blurted. "People end up without a roof for
many reasons—mortgage and rent arrears, the break-
down of relationships, families or friends withdraw-
ing their support. However, it seems that most people

assume that only those suffering from personality difficulties, the onset of mental illness or addiction live on the streets."

"I think I've been guilty of that assumption," she confessed. "Even at the shelter, I have never come into contact with anyone who speaks as eloquently as you. Most are dealing with addiction or a mental illness. I guess I just never really considered that included in the transient population could be people who have lost their homes or jobs."

Ryan decided not to say more for fear that he would give away the ruse. He had probably already said too much. Sage didn't appear to be suspicious of him. Perhaps she just assumed that he was speaking in defense of his current situation.

Their gaze met and held.

Sage broke the visual exchange by saying, "I'll have Franklin get your clothing size." She checked her watch and then said, "I'm afraid I have a meeting to attend, but I'll check on you afterward."

"Thank you for your kindness," Ryan murmured sincerely. "I don't know many people who would go this far for a stranger."

"We shouldn't have to wait for something terrible to happen before we reach out to help others," Sage stated. "My dad used to say this all the time."

"Sounds like your father is a wise man." Malcolm Alexander apparently shared some of the same philosophies as his biological father.

"He is," Sage confirmed. "He also used to say that a true act of kindness happens when there is no reason to be kind but simply out of caring for our fellow man."

Ryan gave a tiny smile. "I like that."

Sage walked toward the door. "I have to go, but I hope you'll enjoy your bath and meal. Franklin will stop by and arrange for some clean clothes for you."

She was gone before Ryan could utter a response.

"Franklin, I wanted to let you know that I placed a guest in unit 210," Sage announced. She called him from her cell phone as soon as she left Ryan.

"Is this a friend of yours?" he politely inquired.

"Not really," Sage answered honestly. "He is someone who has been living on the streets as a transient. He's an educated man, and I'm pretty sure something must have happened in his life for him to be homeless. In a way, he reminds me a lot of you, Franklin."

"I see."

"This is not something that I've done before, but there is something about this man. Franklin, I felt as if I had to do something to help him."

"I understand completely," Franklin responded.

"Do you really?"

"Yes. As you know, I was homeless when Mr. Robert and I met," Franklin reminded her. "Like you, he had a kind heart, and not only did he give me a job but also a place to stay. You and your grandfather are kindred spirits."

"I do feel this connection with Robert," Sage admitted. "I've never said this before because I don't want my family to think I'm losing it."

"There's nothing insane about it," Franklin assured her. "His blood runs in your veins as well as your father's. It's natural that you would possess some of his traits."

"We've been so blessed, Franklin, with all of this. However, even before the inheritance came about, I've never known what it feels like to be hungry or homeless. I volunteer at the homeless shelters and donate, but this time it just didn't seem enough. Once I looked into this guy's eyes, I just had to do something more."

Franklin had served as a butler to Robert DePaul until his death. Her father had no use for butlers, so he promoted Franklin as head of the security and housekeeping staff. He traveled frequently, making sure everything ran smoothly with all of the hotel properties. He often accompanied Malcolm and Ari when they travelled, rarely entrusting them to the care of any other member of the security team.

"If you would see that he has some clean clothes, you can put them on my personal account. I mainly wanted to alert you in the event someone said something about his being here. Please make sure the security team understands that I do not want him harassed in any way. I want Ryan's stay to be a comfortable one."

"Understood. How long will he be staying here?"

"I'm not sure," Sage answered. "I'm hoping we will be able to provide a job for him, as well. But anyway, thanks so much, Franklin. I appreciate all that you do for us."

"It is my pleasure," Franklin responded. "I will head to the second level to introduce myself to your guest. I want him to know that he can contact me if he needs anything."

Sage smiled. "His name is Ryan Manning. Thanks."

Beneath all the grime, Sage could see glimpses of an extremely handsome man. He had not been on the streets long, she decided. He was muscled and strong. Ryan hadn't missed too many meals—that much she was pretty sure of, although she really didn't know much about him.

Sage made it to the conference room minutes before her staff arrived. She wanted to go over the departmental vacation calendar as there had been some recent changes; two of her employees had been promoted to other departments.

"Good afternoon, everyone," she greeted, closing the door so they would not be disturbed or disturb others. Blaze was in the room next door, meeting with his direct reports.

"We need to review the vacation calendar to ensure that we are going to have coverage," she began.

Her meeting lasted for about thirty minutes.

After it was finished, Sage stopped by her office to make a phone call to Personnel. She was interrupted by a visitor.

"Harold, what do you want?" she asked. Although they were related by blood, Sage had a hard time considering him part of her family—especially after the way he tried to manipulate her father.

"I still have friends here," he responded.

"Don't you mean spies?" Sage countered.

Harold chuckled. "You really shouldn't be so paranoid."

"Why are you here, Harold?"

"I would like to make peace with your family," he

announced. "I thought the best person to start with would be you, Sage."

She eyed him hard. "Do you think that I am the weakest link? Because if you do, then I'm afraid I will disappoint you."

"I don't think that you are weak at anything," Harold responded. "There is no escaping the fact that we are related."

"You're right about that," Sage uttered, betraying nothing of her annoyance. She leaned back in her chair, studying Harold DePaul. "There's something you want from me. What is it?"

"My sister Meredith is looking for a job in residential sales. She would really like to work with you in the *family* business."

Sage had only met Meredith once, and very few words were exchanged between them. "Why didn't she come here to talk to me? She's a grown woman. I assume she can speak for herself."

"My sister wasn't sure how she would be received," Harold confessed.

Sage straightened up in her chair, saying, "We are not the reason for the discord amongst Robert DePaul's relatives."

"I am well aware of that, Sage," Harold responded. "We had no idea that Uncle Robert had a son. Surely, you can understand why we were concerned as to what would happen to the estate?"

"To a point," Sage stated. "You do know that you are not going to get off the hook that easily, Harold."

"Let's not make this about me. Are you willing to give my sister a chance? I offered her a job, but as I said, she wants to be a part of Uncle Robert's legacy. She wants to work with you."

"I really have to give this some thought." Sage found it a little hard to swallow that Meredith suddenly wanted to come work with her. She didn't trust Harold as far as she could throw him, but it wasn't fair to judge Meredith by her brother's actions.

"I would like to speak with Meredith. She wants the job, so she'll have to meet with me."

Harold nodded in agreement. "I hope that you will be fair."

"I am always fair," Sage countered. "If you had taken time to get to know me, then you wouldn't be worried."

Harold's smile was without humor.

"What?" Sage asked.

"You remind me of Uncle Robert. You really are a lot like him."

"So I've been told," she responded.

Harold checked his watch and then rose to his feet. "I appreciate you taking time to speak with me, Sage. I'll have Meredith contact you."

"I look forward to speaking to her."

He paused at the door. "I do hope that one day we can really put the past behind us."

"It starts with you, Harold."

"Enjoy the rest of your day, Sage."

"You do the same," she responded.

They exchanged a polite, simultaneous smile and then Harold was gone.

Sage wasn't sure what to think of her conversation with Harold. However, she decided to withhold judgment until she had a chance to meet with Meredith. A small part of her considered that this was a way for Harold to plant someone in her department, but he would soon find that she was not one to be reckoned with.

Her thoughts traveled to Ryan Manning. Franklin should have dropped off clothes and clean undergarments by now. She decided to give him more time to make himself presentable. Sage made a few phone calls to pass the time.

She was looking forward to seeing him again.

This is so crazy, she thought. *Why do I feel such a strong connection with this man?*

Am I so desperate that I'd be interested in a homeless man?

Sage thought about R. G. McCall's article and shook her head in despair.

Chapter 6

When Franklin showed up at the door of Ryan's hotel room with a shopping bag overflowing with clothing, he surveyed the man from head to toe. If he was suspicious, he kept his thoughts to himself.

"Ms. Alexander thought you would be more comfortable in these," he told Ryan upon entering into the room.

Sage had been honest about Franklin coming to the suite to check Ryan out. For whatever reason, she wanted a second opinion on him.

It didn't really bother Ryan.

"You haven't been on the streets very long," Franklin commented. "You should consider yourself very lucky to have found favor with Ms. Alexander. She has elected to become your guardian angel."

"I am very grateful," Ryan stated.

"Where are you from?" Franklin inquired. "I would guess New York."

"You would be correct," Ryan responded. "You have an ear for accents, I see."

"How did you come to be in Los Angeles?"

Ryan knew that his story had to be a good one. "I moved out here to start a business. I used to be a chef and I wanted my own restaurant. Turns out, running a business like that is much harder than I thought. I lost my business and my home when I filed bankruptcy. Moved to Los Angeles to start over and was living in my car until it got impounded. I haven't been able to really find a job, so I don't have the money get the car back. Been on the streets ever since then."

"I've been there," Franklin said. "I certainly understand when you're in the midst of a storm. The Alexander family is nice people, and they care about others. Some people will try to take advantage of them, but I intend to do everything in my power to make sure it doesn't happen."

"Understood," Ryan said.

Franklin left the suite a few minutes later.

Ryan removed the plush hotel robe and put on the clothing. Franklin had called the room to verify sizes before making his purchases, so everything fit perfectly.

Ten minutes later, there was a soft knock on the door.

He was thrilled to see Sage standing there but buried his true feelings.

Ryan could feel Sage's eyes studying him. He kept his gaze glued to the floor, not wanting to give up his ruse.

"Great, you're all dressed," she said. "I hope that you're pleased with Franklin's selections."

"He could have brought me a paper bag, and I would be appreciative," Ryan stated.

Sage grinned, silently noting how handsome he looked in the crisp, white shirt and black denim jeans.

Oh, my goodness! This man is so gorgeous.

She gestured toward the sofa and asked if they could talk.

Ryan allowed her to lead the way and took a seat.

"I hope you don't think that I'm being too nosy, but I'm curious. I can tell that you haven't been on the streets very long."

"Why do you say that?" Ryan wanted to know.

"You don't look like the other homeless people," she responded. "I volunteer at one of the homeless shelters, so I'm around the homeless a lot."

Ryan recalled that Sage volunteered at one of the shelters. There were many facets to her and he wanted to get to know them all.

His eyes drank in her beauty.

"How did you come to this road in your life?" she inquired softly, drawing Ryan's attention back to their conversation.

He repeated what he had told Franklin.

"I'm so sorry," Sage murmured. "I'm sure this has been a very difficult time for you."

"It has," Ryan responded. "But I've never been a quitter."

"I'm so glad to hear that," she said. "So you know how to cook?"

He nodded. "Apparently not good enough to keep my restaurant afloat, though."

"What type of restaurant did you own?"

"Southern, believe it or not. I grew up in New Orleans. I specialized in authentic Southern cooking."

"How would you cook shrimp and grits?" Sage questioned.

He looked surprised by her inquiry but answered anyway. "I'd take yellow stone-ground grits, milk, onion, butter and extra virgin olive oil." He grinned. "Can't forget the shrimp."

"You make the ingredients sound yummy," Sage told Ryan. "Do you know how to make seafood gumbo?"

"I may have a New York accent, but my heart belongs to my New Orleans roots. I know how to make gumbo, jambalaya, crawfish étouffée and po'boys." He met her gaze. "Why do you ask?"

"We're opening a new restaurant here in the hotel," she announced. "Le Magnifique was born from a passionate desire to offer an authentic dining experience that far exceeded the average 'hotel restaurant' offering of today. Our goal is to serve up a Louisiana flavor because we believe such fare has broad appeal and can be both comfort food as well as a gourmet experience for our guests. We want a delicious combination of Louisiana cuisines, incorporating Cajun, Bayou, Creole and other local cultural tastes and ingredients. We are looking for someone to manage it. After talking to you, I believe that we've found one."

Ryan didn't bother to hide his surprise. "Are you offering me a job?"

Sage smiled and nodded. "I still have to run it by my parents and my brother Ari, but I am sure it's a done deal—that is, if you want the job."

Ryan shook his head in disbelief.

"You don't want it?" Sage asked.

"Oh, no, that's not what… Ms. Alexander…" Ryan searched for the right words. "I'm just surprised."

"You've been through a lot, Ryan. What I'm offering you is a second chance."

"I accept, Ms. Alexander."

"It's just Sage," she corrected. "Oh, and you have to meet with my brother Ari. He is the general manager."

"Sage, I can't thank you enough for all you've done for me."

"I can move you into one of the staff rooms until you can find a place of your own. We may be able to give you an advance on your salary after you've been here for ninety days. I'd like for you to meet with Donna in Personnel tomorrow morning. I'll give her a call to let her know to expect you."

She smiled at Ryan before leaving the hotel suite.

The warmth of her smile sent a rush of heat through him.

She is a temptation I cannot afford.

Ryan had to remind himself that he was in Los Angeles to work on his investigative piece. There was no time for romancing the beautiful and caring heiress. He had made it a practice to never get emotionally involved with anyone connected to his research for fear of tainting his work. Ryan had expected to be able to observe the Alexander family from a distance and through interviews with others, but Sage changed all this when she gave him the hundred-dollar bill and offered him this suite and now employment.

He felt a shard of guilt where Sage was concerned. He didn't like misleading her, but it was necessary for his article.

* * *

Meredith DePaul was waiting for Sage outside her office. She had not expected to see the young woman so soon.

"My brother told me that you wanted to meet with me."

"He's correct," Sage responded. "I thought it was best for the two of us to talk, since you want to work with me. This will give me a chance to get to know you."

Meredith followed her into the office. She took a seat in one of the visitor chairs without waiting for an invitation. "What do you want to know?"

"Anything you want to tell me," Sage responded.

"Well, I graduated from UCLA with a degree in business. I have my real estate license, and I used to work here at the hotel when I was in college. Although Uncle Robert left the hotels to your father, they are still a part of my legacy. I am a part of this family, and I want to work in the family business."

Meredith brushed away a dark curl from her face. "Tell me something. Why are you here?"

"My story is very similar to yours. I want to work with my family. It is important to make some things clear, Meredith. We did not steal this business from you or your family. Robert DePaul made his wishes known in an ironclad will. I hope we will not have to rehash this over and over. We have no problem embracing the DePaul relatives, but we will not be manipulated or defrauded in any manner."

"We don't," Meredith responded. "Now, I'd like to be just as honest. I am not coming here to spy on you or your family. If you don't want me here in Beverly Hills, I'm willing to relocate to one of the other properties."

"What is your preference?"

Meredith didn't flinch. "I'd like to stay here and learn from you. Despite everything that happened between my brother and your father, I feel that we would make a dynamic team."

A smile tugged at Sage's lips.

"It is also a great way to diminish any awkwardness between us. We're related, and nothing will ever change that. I can't pretend that you don't exist, Sage. I have to admit that I'm curious about you and your family. I want to get to know all of you."

"You can do that without working with us."

"I know that," Meredith countered. "But I also want to work in this business. I loved working at the hotel."

"I need to speak with my parents and Ari," Sage stated. "Can I give you a call later today?"

"Sure."

Meredith headed toward the door but paused long enough to say, "I hope that you won't judge me by my brother's actions."

"I think you'll find that we are willing to give others a chance even if they are not willing to do the same."

As soon as Meredith left her office, Sage made a quick phone call to Ari.

She gave him a summary of her conversation with Harold and then with Meredith. "So what do you think?"

"I don't trust Harold at all," Ari stated. "I'm not sure I trust his sister either."

"Meredith is our cousin," Sage reminded him. "She wants to work in the family business."

"She is coming here to either spy on us or try and sabotage us in some way."

"I don't think so," Sage countered. "I talked to her, and I believe she is sincere."

"I think your instincts are off this time, sis."

"Meredith is willing to relocate if need be, Ari. I really don't think she has the same motives as Harold."

Ari released an audible sigh. "I have to be honest with you, Sage. I'm not comfortable with this at all. She can still try to sabotage us from another location."

"Let's run it by Daddy and see what he has to say about Meredith coming to work with me," Sage suggested. "I'll go with whatever he decides."

"Fair enough," Ari responded.

"Oh, one more thing," Sage stated. "I've found a manager for the new restaurant."

"Really? Who is it?"

"Ryan Manning. He used to be a chef and had his own business in New York. But get this—he was born and raised in New Orleans. Having someone like him on staff will ensure that the food we serve will be authentic."

"When did you find him?" Ari inquired.

Sage did not respond. She was searching for the right way to tell her brother that she had discovered Ryan on the streets.

"Sage…" Ari prompted.

"I met Ryan on the streets," she blurted. "He was homeless."

"Excuse me?"

"I have a good feeling about him," Sage quickly interjected. "He's been through so much—losing his business and his home, filing bankruptcy and then living in his car until it was impounded. That's a lot to endure, don't you think? Besides, Franklin talked to him and he feels the same as I do. This is someone who is going through a really tough time."

"Sis, you can't save the world."

"I'm not trying to save everyone—just this one guy and because I strongly believe that he deserves a chance."

"First Meredith and now some homeless man," Ari uttered with a shake of his head. "I don't know how Dad is going to handle this news."

"Just trust me on this," Sage pleaded. "Ryan is the perfect man for the position of manager. As for Meredith…I'm willing to give her a chance."

"I need to meet Ryan. I'd like to be able to tell Dad something more about him other than he used to be homeless."

"I told him that you would have to meet him," Sage responded. "Thank you, Ari."

"Don't thank me, Sage. I'm going on record that I'm not sure about any of this, but I am going to trust your instincts."

When Sage hung up the phone, she leaned back in her chair and smiled. Ari would soon come to see that her instincts were on point when it came to Ryan.

Sage Alexander is an incredible woman.

The thought played in Ryan's head over and over again. She had just handed him a management position within the hotel just on faith alone. Her brother did not seem as thrilled about her decision, however.

Ryan had just spent the past half hour in a conference room with Ari Alexander, the general manager. He had undergone an intense interview session, but Ryan was okay with it. He walked out of the room feeling positive that he had sealed the bid for the management position. This was not how he had planned to get his story, but Ryan intended to roll with it. Working for the Alexander family provided a more intimate view of their lives.

Of course, he had to prepare a full course meal later today for Sage, Ari and their father, along with the chef of the other restaurant, according to the HR consultant. He had to undergo a drug test and background check, which didn't bother Ryan. He had been honest for the most part, except his business was not failing and he had never experienced bankruptcy.

Ryan had learned from a member of the waitstaff that Sage loved fish and pasta. He already knew what he was going to prepare and had given the kitchen staff a list of ingredients needed for the meal.

He was on his way toward the hotel lobby when he spotted Sage in the company of a man and woman. Ryan assumed that she was about to show them one of the penthouse units. He stopped in his tracks, his gaze traveling from her face to her curves. She was smiling as she talked with them. It was genuine and not one of those fake "I'll do anything to make this sale" smiles.

She caught sight of him and gave a slight nod.

Even in the midst of her job, she took a brief pause to acknowledge him. Ryan smiled to himself. He was beginning to think that she was the real deal.

However, there was still much more to learn about her and the rest of her family. If things continued along this vein, this story was going to be a pleasure to write, he told himself. It was time for some news that would leave readers feeling hopeful and inspired to take action.

Chapter 7

Sage sat with her father and Ari at a table in the new restaurant. The head chef from Café Rodeo joined them a few minutes later. Although Ryan was being considered for manager, they all wanted to make sure that he had cooking experience and knew how to run a kitchen.

Malcolm had listened quietly as Sage discussed why she wanted to help Ryan. When she was done, her father met her gaze and asked, "You feel this strongly about hiring this man?"

"I do," she responded.

Before they could continue their conversation, the appetizers came out. Sage sampled the blue crab with wild mushroom ravioli and served with a peppercorn cream sauce. "This is absolutely delicious," she gushed.

"I have to agree, sis," Ari said. "In fact, I'd like to add this to our menu."

Malcolm and Chef David agreed.

Ryan had surprised them all when he presented not one but three entrées for them to taste. The first was a boneless, skinless chicken breast served atop new-potato mash and steamed asparagus.

"The chicken can also be topped with lump crabmeat and tasso hollandaise," Ryan stated.

The second entrée of shrimp and andouille sausage poached in a Creole meunière reduction and served over grits was an instant hit with Sage. "I don't know about you, but I am one hundred percent positive that I've found the right man for the job," she said to Ari in a low voice.

The third entrée served by Ryan was sliced tenderloin of beef that had been lightly charred and cooked to perfection, accompanied by a béarnaise sauce, mashed potatoes and asparagus. This one was her father's favorite of the three.

It was another entrée they should feature on their new menu, Sage decided.

Ryan followed up with dessert. He had prepared bread pudding with a whiskey sauce.

She smiled and nodded in approval.

He was a great cook. Sage was glad to see he sought to impress her father and brother by going above and beyond by preparing three separate entrées. She thought he had made excellent choices in deciding to feature white meat, red meat and seafood. It was brilliant on Ryan's part.

It was still hard to understand why his life had taken such a downward spiral, but he had not let it get the better of him. Sage was impressed with the man standing before them. He didn't look afraid or nervous; there was a calm about him. He was very comfortable in his own skin.

Her father had Ryan join them at the table. Sage felt strongly that Ryan's life was about to change for the better.

Ryan's eyes traveled slowly around the room, taking in the interior of the Le Magnifique restaurant. He was now the manager of this exquisite new venture. Unlike most restaurants, which have only one central dining room, Le Magnifique had two—one tucked away in a corner, designed for guests seeking a private and intimate dining experience. Celebrities and other VIPs, who desired to enjoy a meal without being disturbed, would most likely use that one.

"I thought I'd find you here," Sage said as she walked up to him. "Well, it's official. You are the new manager of Le Magnifique."

"None of this would be possible if it hadn't been for you."

She smiled at him. "You deserve it, Ryan. Everything you prepared tonight was delicious. You are a wonderful cook. I hate to admit this, but you're much better than I am."

"Where is your father and brother?" Ryan asked. "I can't remember if I thanked them for giving me this chance."

"Ari went upstairs, and my dad is on his way home. You did thank them."

Ryan glanced around the restaurant once more. "I still can't believe it. My life has changed a lot over a short period of time."

"We were destined to meet," Sage stated. "I really believe that. When I saw you the first time, all I could think of was that I had to do something to help this man."

"I want you to know that I am glad I had a chance to meet you, Ms. Alexander."

"I look forward to a long working relationship," Sage responded with a smile. "Security is waiting to lock up, so I guess we need to get out of here."

There was no denying that he was attracted to her, but Ryan tried to shake the idea out of his mind. Acting on his attraction would be a huge mistake.

They walked out of the restaurant together.

"I'm going to start looking for a place to live," Ryan blurted. "I don't want to wear out my welcome here."

"You are more than welcome to stay here for as long as necessary, Ryan. We have some guest rooms that are only for staff. However, I understand if you want some place to call your own, so let me know if I can do anything to help."

He laughed. "I can't afford the type of properties you represent."

"You never know," Sage countered. "You may be able to do so in the future."

Ryan gave her a sidelong glance. "Are you always so positive?"

Sage managed a tremulous smile. "I try to be."

"I like that."

"If you'd like me to, I can pull some rentals for you."

"That would be nice," Ryan responded. "I appreciate your help."

He grew quiet for a moment, prompting Sage to ask, "You okay?"

Ryan nodded. "I'm just not used to having anyone look out for me like this. Franklin called you my guardian angel. He's right."

"I'm no angel," Sage responded with a short laugh.

"You are my angel."

Her gaze was riveted to his face. Sage found herself extremely cognizant of Ryan's virile appeal. The smoldering flame she saw in Ryan's eyes fascinated her. Her eyes traveled to his full lips that left her wondering what it would be like to feel those lips against her own.

She cleared her throat softly. "I need to... I have to meet my brother for lunch."

Sage thought she glimpsed a shimmer of disappointment in Ryan's eyes, but it was gone as quickly as it had appeared.

He walked her to the private elevator. "I owe you a debt of gratitude, Sage. I intend to repay that debt."

"Just do the best job you can, and that will be payment enough." She refused to look at him this time because all she could think about was how her body ached for his touch and his kissable lips.

Ryan could not ignore the tingling in the pit of his stomach.

His feelings for Sage were intensifying. Everything around him seemed to take on a clean brightness whenever she was around.

"This is insane," he muttered. "I can't have these kinds of feelings for Sage."

Ryan was only in town to work his story. After all

Sage had done for him, he felt guilty for misleading her. He had even taken a job as restaurant manager. This was probably the craziest move yet.

He silently reasoned that he had to continue to play along to keep Sage from becoming suspicious. How could he explain turning down a job?

Ryan vowed to keep a professional distance where Sage was concerned. He had to continue this charade until he had all the material he needed to write his article.

A wave of sadness flushed through him. Ryan had not felt such an intense attraction toward anyone like this in a long time. He kept telling himself that his feelings for Sage had nothing to do with reason.

The truth was that she had brought senses to life that Ryan thought were long dead.

Ryan left the hotel and walked the surrounding area.

Three blocks from the hotel, Ryan noticed a scrap of dirty blanket visible under some stairs and a bag of recyclables parked discreetly behind a bush. To most people, it looked like trash, but he had learned how to decode the bits of urban detritus that most people ignored. That area beneath the stairs was someone's home.

He moved closer.

There was an elderly woman sound asleep beneath a worn, tattered sheet.

"Ma'am," Ryan said gently.

Startled, she opened her eyes and sat up, cowering in fear.

"I'm sorry," Ryan said. "I didn't mean to scare you. I just wanted to make sure that you're okay."

"What do you care?" she sniped.

"I care a lot," he responded.

Ryan pulled out his wallet and showed her his driver's license. "I'm a writer, and I'm working on a piece about homelessness." He took out a fifty dollar bill. "I'd like to ask you some questions, if you don't mind."

"You got that in smaller bills?" the woman asked.

"I have two tens, two fives and a twenty. Will this do?"

She nodded and whispered, "I can hide the money in different places—people steal, you know."

"I understand."

She accepted the money with a toothless grin. "What do you want to know? It really don't matter what I tell you, though. Nobody can know what it is like until they've lived one night out here."

Ryan agreed with her. The time he spent actually sleeping on the streets and in the shelter was a very different life and not for the faint at heart.

"I always have to worry about gang members or that the police will come and make me move. It sometimes gets real cold at night."

"What's your story?" Ryan asked.

"You mean what's my truth," she countered.

He smiled. "Yes, ma'am. That's exactly what I mean."

"Ma'am…humph…you make me sound like a lady and not some lump on the sidewalk."

"What is your name?"

"I'd rather keep that to myself, but you can call me Lady Tee."

"Okay, Lady Tee. What is your truth?"

"I lost everything I had in a fire. We let our insurance lapse because we thought that we didn't need it.

Our house was paid for and wasn't much, but it belonged to me and my husband."

"Where is your husband?"

"He died in the fire. He got me out and went back in to try to save our pictures. I told him to just stay with me, but he wouldn't listen."

"I'm so sorry," Ryan stated.

She shrugged in nonchalance. "It was a long time ago."

"Do you have any family?"

Lady Tee shook her head no. "My husband and I never had any children."

"What about the shelter?"

"Every time I go there, I wake up to find my stuff missing. I used to have some battery-operated baby monitors as a burglar alarm, but somebody stole them, too. I can't afford to lose nothing else, so I stay by myself." Lady Tee pointed to a stack of books. "I am rebuilding my library. I love to read romance novels. They make me feel good."

Ryan smiled. "I love the written word myself. I can certainly understand why they are so precious to you."

He sat and talked with Lady Tee for almost an hour.

"Thank you for taking time out to speak with me."

She grinned. "God bless you for what you are trying to do."

Ryan smiled in return, but deep down he felt as if it was not enough.

As he walked, Ryan mentally went over the information he had uncovered thus far. He discovered that scores of homeless people built semipermanent homes in the chaparral-covered hills that rise above the Hollywood

Bowl. Hundreds lived in Griffith Park and Elysian Park and on islands in the Los Angeles River.

Ryan recalled a few years back that homeless people were discovered living above a concrete channel along the 405 Freeway. He never really understood why some people preferred to sleep in remote places by themselves while others grouped together in places like Skid Row or Hollywood. Lady Tee had given him some perspective on this.

On the way back to the hotel, Ryan encountered another homeless person who identified himself only as Simon.

Ryan engaged him in conversation by offering him the fifty dollar bill. Simon had no problem accepting the money—a sign that he wasn't worried about being robbed.

"I usually prefer to sleep in Griffith Park," Simon explained, "but I come up here during the week so that I can be available for jobs early in the morning."

He showed Ryan his shaving kit. "I always try to look presentable, despite my situation." In addition to the shaving kit, Simon's worldly possessions included two blankets, a battery-operated black-and-white TV and a set of headphones. He did not want to disturb others who may be sleeping around him.

Simon ended the interview by saying, "To survive on the streets, it is necessary to live by a different set of rules. Ryan, where would you sleep if you were homeless?" he asked.

Ryan let the question go unanswered.

Chapter 8

Meredith met her brother for lunch at a nearby restaurant.

When they were seated at a table, Harold asked, "How do you enjoy working for Sage?"

"She's actually very nice," Meredith answered. "Sage definitely knows her job. I have to admit that I have learned a lot from her already. She has a generous spirit. Everyone at the hotel is talking about the homeless man she brought in, and now he's the manager of the new restaurant."

"You can't be serious?" Harold DePaul uttered with disgust. "What is she thinking—bringing some strange man off the street?"

"She appears to be a lot like Uncle Robert. Remember, he brought in Franklin when he was homeless."

"My uncle was fortunate that Franklin did not rob him blind or kill him in his sleep. We can't say the same about this man she's picked up off the streets. If Malcolm cannot control his daughter's antics, then I will intervene. I want to know everything about this man—who he is and where he comes from." Harold picked up his menu.

"I'm not going to be your spy," Meredith stated firmly. "I told you that from the beginning."

"I thought you cared about the DePaul legacy."

She met her brother's gaze. "I do, but I am not about to start another Alexander-DePaul feud."

He shook his head in frustration. "I'll take care of this myself. I'll call Adam Hastings and have him check out this man. He is the best detective for this job."

"Just make sure you don't do anything to ruin this for me, Harold," Meredith warned. "I intend to make sure my hands remain clean." She laid down her menu. "Instead of being on opposite sides, why don't you try to get to know them?"

Ryan picked up a discarded copy of the *Los Angeles Times*. He scanned through the paper, pausing when he spied a familiar face.

Sandra was getting married again.

Ryan's mouth tightened. It wasn't that he was still in love with his ex-wife, because that was not the case. He still harbored resentment in his heart for the way their marriage ended.

She had somehow lied and manipulated her way into another marriage—this time to a movie producer.

The memory of finding Sandra's birth control pills floated through his mind. At the time, Ryan was looking forward to becoming a father. If she was not ready, then all she had to do was be honest with him. However, when he confronted Sandra, she confessed that she didn't want children at all.

Ryan drew himself out of the past. It was time to focus on the here and now.

He called Paige to check on her and Cassie and then decided to go visit them. Paige sounded a little down on the phone, so he wanted to make sure she was okay.

Ryan left the hotel and hailed a taxi.

Fifteen minutes later, he was dropped off at the little motel where Paige had been staying.

He knocked on the door, and then said, "It's me, Ryan."

Paige peeked out of the window before throwing the door open.

"Ryan?" Paige's eyes stayed on his face for a moment before traveling downward, taking in the new clothes, his clean-shaven appearance. "Wow..."

"How are things with you?" he asked Paige.

"I still can't find a job."

"I had some luck in that department," Ryan announced. "I'm the new manager of the Le Magnifique restaurant in the Alexander-DePaul Hotel."

"That's wonderful, Ryan." She embraced him. "I'm so happy for you."

"I'm going to check to see what positions they have available. Maybe we can find something for you to do."

"I hope so. I cannot keep depending on you. Although I don't know how you've been able to do so much."

"I'm resourceful," Ryan responded with a tiny smile.

"Then you need to teach me how to be so resourceful because I'm failing miserably."

"Don't lose hope, Paige. Everything is going to work out."

"For you maybe," she responded. "I'm not worried so much about myself. It's Cassie. I don't want her taken from me because I can't support her right now."

"That won't happen," Ryan stated firmly. "I'd never let that happen."

"I'm so glad that you're my friend. I've never met anyone like you, Ryan."

The baby started to stir.

Paige picked her up. "Look, Cassie. Look who is here to see you. It's Uncle Ryan."

The little girl smiled at him.

His heart warmed at the sight of her sweet smile. Ryan reached for her. "C'mere cutie. Every time I see your face, you make my day so much brighter."

As he played with Cassie, Ryan thought about another female who made his days light up with her smile.

Sage and her siblings decided to spend the weekend with their parents at the Pacific Palisades estate. Her parents had opted to stay in the house instead of the penthouse at the hotel because they preferred the solace and quiet of the house over the hustle and bustle of living in the hotel. Her parents were planning to give Ari and Natasha the penthouse as a wedding gift.

They were all outside on the patio with her parents. Malcolm and Blaze were working the grill, while Barbara sat nearby engaged in conversation with Natasha. Drayden had brought a date with him, and they were in the swimming pool.

Hearing laughter, Sage turned around in the lounge

chair. Ari was teaching Joshua how to swim in the shallow end of the pool. She was thrilled to see her brother happy again. She had worried that he would never be the same after he lost his first love, April. However, Natasha and Joshua entered his life when he needed them the most. Ari had formally adopted Joshua, who was in remission after a bout with leukemia. The two were as close as any father and son.

"Good job," Ari told Joshua. "You're going to be swimming on your own in no time."

"Yeah," the little boy responded. "Hey, Mommy, watch me. I'm swimming."

"I see you," Natasha said. "I'm so proud of you."

Blaze strode over and sat down beside Sage, saying, "Ari is really good with him."

She agreed. "I always knew he'd be a good father. Remember how he used to treat us like we were his children?"

Chuckling, Blaze nodded.

"How about you?" Sage asked. "Do you want children someday?"

"Yeah, I do," he responded. "I wouldn't mind having a son and a daughter."

"Two children? You really want to have two kids?"

He laughed. "I don't know, Sage. I'll have to see how it goes with the first one."

"Auntie Sage, did you see me swim?" Joshua asked, running up to her chair. He was dripping wet and grinning from ear to ear.

"I did," Sage responded as she dried him off with a fluffy towel. Joshua had stolen her heart the first time she ever met him. She spent as much time with him as she could.

"What about you, Uncle B?"

Blaze nodded. "Good job, little man."

"Are we still gonna do something special together?" Joshua asked Blaze, who nodded a second time.

"We sure are—just you and me."

Ari got out of the pool and stood up, toweling off his body. "Joshua, c'mon. It's time for a bath."

"Okaay," he responded with a sigh.

Sage hid her smile. She watched as Ari took Joshua by the hand and headed inside the house.

"Your brother is a wonderful father," Natasha murmured as she sat down beside Sage. "Joshua adores him. You should have seen the two of them yesterday. Ari was teaching him to play checkers."

Sage smiled. "Daddy taught Ari how to play when he was Joshua's age."

"I love watching the two of them together," Natasha stated. "I really value the time they spend together and cherish the memories they are creating."

Twenty minutes later, Ari and Joshua returned, joining everyone on the patio.

They sat down to feast on hamburgers, homemade potato salad and hot dogs. "We'll be back in a couple of hours," Ari announced when he and Joshua had finished eating.

"Where are you two going?" Natasha asked from across the table.

"I promised Joshua that we would get ice cream after dinner."

"Yum," Natasha responded with a grin. "Are you going to bring some back to me?"

Laughing, Joshua shook his head no. "I'm going to eat it all."

Natasha pretended to be sad.

This sent Joshua into more laughter.

"Now, Joshua, I know you're going to bring some ice cream back for all of us because I know how much you love to share," Natasha said.

He nodded. "I'm gonna share. I was just teasing, Mommy."

Joshua ran over to his mother and planted a kiss on his mother's lips. "I love you."

"I love you, too, son."

Sage's eyes teared up, watching the two of them. Like her brother Blaze, she wanted at least two children. Of course, she needed to find a husband first.

Chapter 9

Monday morning, Ryan was up early and training with the manager of the other hotel restaurant. He was actually looking forward to running Le Magnifique. It would provide a stimulating challenge for him.

He was thrilled to see Sage when she walked into the restaurant. She looked stunning in the red-and-black dress she was wearing. He was entranced by her compelling personage.

"How is it going?" she asked.

"Good," Ryan responded. He had not seen her since Friday and missed her beautiful smile. "Dan is a great trainer. I am not really an auditory learner, so he is allowing me to gain hands-on experience. I've picked up some great tips from him."

He was actually going to institute some of what he learned from Dan into his own restaurant management.

Sage looked as if she were trying to find something to say.

She released a nervous laugh before saying, "I'm glad to hear that things are going so well."

Every time Sage's gaze met his, her heart turned over in response. Ryan really liked her and wanted to get to know her better. However, he wasn't sure he could keep from connecting with Sage on a personal level.

She had gotten under his skin, and Ryan was powerless to resist.

"Are you busy right now?" he asked.

"No," she responded. "What's up?"

"Would you have lunch with me?" Ryan blurted. "You've done so much for me. At least let me buy you lunch."

"Sure," Sage told him.

They decided to leave the hotel property and walked down the street to a restaurant.

Sage seemed nervous at first, but once they were seated at a table, she appeared more like herself.

"Does it bother you to be seen with me?" Ryan asked.

Shaking her head, she frowned. "Why would you ask me that?"

"You seemed a little apprehensive earlier. I know that you and your family don't need to have to deal with the kind of tabloid news that could come from just being seen with me. I'm sure someone at the hotel is going to connect the dots where I'm concerned."

"I really don't care what other people think. I just don't want the media hounding you in any way," she told him, but did not elaborate any further.

Ryan didn't press her. He was touched that she was trying to protect him.

The waiter arrived to take their drink orders.

He observed her discreetly. Ryan couldn't tear his gaze from her profile.

She glanced up from her menu. "So tell me, Ryan, what do you do for fun?"

"I enjoy reading. In fact, I really enjoy mysteries and nonfiction—mostly on African American history."

"Interesting," she murmured. "I'm a reader as well, but my tastes lend more to contemporary women's fiction."

Their waiter returned with their drinks.

Sage took a sip of her iced tea. "I like some nonfiction, but they tend to be self-improvement books."

"I love history myself. In fact, I'm reading a book on the history of Allensworth."

"Allensworth?" Sage repeated. "What is Allensworth?"

"Colonel Allen Allensworth established an all-Black community in the southwest corner of Tulare County. The township had a depot station on the main Santa Fe Railroad line from Los Angeles to San Francisco."

"I've never heard anything about it," Sage said. "This is very interesting."

Ryan smiled. "It is interesting. The 1912 to 1915 period marked the apex of Allensworth as a thriving community. African American newspapers throughout the nation chronicled its growth. Even the *Los Angeles Times* took note of the township. They called it the ideal Negro settlement."

Their meals arrived.

Sage and Ryan continued discussing the history of Allensworth. He was pleased to find someone who shared his interest in African American history. Sandra was never interested in anything connected to history, books or anything Ryan seemed to enjoy.

Did we ever have anything in common outside of sex? he wondered. Their relationship was mostly a physical one; there was never a friendship between the two.

Ryan brought his attention back to Sage.

He could read the excitement in her eyes as they discussed other areas across America where there had once been African American towns.

Ryan had not dated much since his marriage ended; instead, he decided to place all of his focus on his work. In just a short period, Sage had begun to threaten that concentration, filling his mind with thoughts of her.

Sage had enjoyed her lunch with Ryan immensely. Sage did an online search for Allensworth as soon as she returned to her office. She wanted to learn more about the town.

She was so caught up in her reading that she hadn't realized she was not alone.

Meredith cleared her throat noisily.

Sage glanced up. "Oh, I'm sorry. Did you need to speak to me?"

"Yes." Meredith sat down in one of the visitor's chairs. "I just spent the past half hour with a couple who decided to buy unit 809. They want to put down a million-dollar deposit and close in fifteen days."

"Really?"

Smiling, Meredith nodded.

"Congratulations," Sage said. "You've already had your first sale and you haven't been here a month yet."

"I'm super excited."

When Meredith left the office, Sage went back to reading about Allensworth.

"I hope you're working hard."

She glanced away from the computer monitor. "Daddy, what are you doing here?"

"Checking in to see how things are going," he responded.

"Everything is fine," Sage stated. "Meredith just had her first sale. Ryan is doing well with the restaurant. The grand opening is all set to happen on time, too. I'm sure Ari told you all of this already, though. Well, except about Meredith, because this just happened."

Malcolm took a seat. "I wanted to tell you that you were right."

Sage met her father's gaze. "About what?"

"Ryan. He has proven to be a major asset to our company. He works hard, that one."

Sage smiled. "He's very intelligent. I had lunch with Ryan earlier, and he was telling me about Allensworth, an African American town not too far from here."

Malcolm studied her face. "You and Ryan getting pretty close, it seems."

"Why do you say that?" she asked, her guard going up immediately.

"You seem to spend a lot of time together."

"He doesn't have any friends here in California. I enjoy Ryan's company, and I don't see anything wrong with getting to know him."

Malcolm held up a hand in defense. "Sugar, I didn't

say anything was wrong with it. I just want you to be careful. This guy works here, and it's not good sense to mix business and pleasure."

"I know that, Daddy. But you don't have to worry about me. I intend to use my head and not my heart where Ryan is concerned."

Chapter 10

The dark clouds looming ominously over Beverly Hills and fifteen miles per hour winds matched Ryan's mood. In a couple of hours, his ex-wife would be another man's wife. On a brighter note, Ryan reminded himself that he would no longer have to give Sandra alimony. There would not be any more ties to her, and for that, he should be happy.

It was Saturday, and Ryan was in his new office, going over menu items. Malcolm and Ari wanted to finalize the menu so that they could get the project over to the printer.

"Knock…knock…"

Ryan glanced up from the computer monitor. "Sage. Come in."

She stopped in her tracks. "What's wrong?"

He seemed surprised by her question.

"You look upset about something," Sage explained.

Ryan had not realized that Sage could read him so well. "It's not important," he responded.

"I'm a good listener." She sat down on the suede sofa.

He gave her a small smile. "Seriously, I'm okay."

"I came in here to see if you like ice cream."

Ryan laughed. "Sure. I like ice cream. May I ask why?"

"I've been thinking of hosting an ice cream social. I'm hosting an open house this weekend, and I thought it would be nice for the kids while their parents are touring the residences. I ordered all sorts of toppings, so I came to see if you would like to experiment with me." She laughed. "Not with me per se, but trying the different toppings..."

He threw back his head laughing. "I know what you meant, Sage."

"So, do you want ice cream?"

"I could use a break right now," he told her. Ryan had a feeling that Sage was trying to cheer him up. She was very intuitive, and he could not deny that her attempt was working.

They took the elevator to her penthouse unit.

"How's the menu coming along?" she inquired.

"It's pretty much done," Ryan responded. "I just have to finalize a couple of things before I send it on to Ari and your father. Upon their approval, it will go straight to the printer.

"What are those?" he asked, pointing to the bottles sitting on the granite kitchen countertop.

"Gourmet dessert toppings," she responded. "Ryan, you should try them. We have chocolate raspberry, chocolate peanut butter crème, white chocolate delight, strawberry vanilla, butter caramel and an orange dream topping."

"They all sound delicious," he said. "They just couldn't offer plain vanilla, chocolate, strawberry or caramel?"

Sage laughed. "They may all be plain with fancy names. This is why we're going to sample them."

Her breath caught in her throat as she met his gaze. Ryan made her heart skip a beat.

Looking away from him, she said, "I'll get some bowls and the ice cream."

When she returned, they sat at the counter and scooped ice cream into their bowls. Sage decided to try the chocolate peanut butter topping with vanilla ice cream. She sprinkled peanuts on top, too.

Ryan chose to try the strawberry over chocolate ice cream. He sprinkled Oreo cookie crumbs over his.

"I guess you're playing it safe," he told her. "See… this is more daring."

Sage made a face. "Yours doesn't look that appetizing."

He stuck a spoonful into his mouth. "It's good."

She grinned. "I don't believe you."

Ryan laughed. "Seriously, try it. It's not bad at all. Do you like chocolate-covered strawberries?"

Sage nodded. "But not with Oreo cookie crumbs." His nearness was overwhelming. There seemed to be some tangible bond between them; it was something she could not ignore. Sage wondered if Ryan felt it, as well.

After they sampled a few more toppings, Ryan offered to help Sage clean up.

"Sage, I hope I'm not about to make a fool of myself, but would you be interested in having dinner with me tonight?"

She looked up at him, and her heart lurched madly. "Okay, just so I'm clear. Is this a friend date or a *date* date?"

Duh…

He nodded. "I hope I'm not being inappropriate. You're not my direct report, so I thought it might be okay."

"It's fine," Sage assured him. "I'd love to have dinner with you."

"I should have probably asked if you were seeing someone. Are you?"

"I'm single," Sage interjected.

"I'm glad to hear it. I have wanted to ask you out for a while now." Ryan checked his watch. "I guess I need to get back to my office. Sage, thanks for the ice cream and the conversation. I enjoyed both." She had been a welcomed distraction for Ryan, especially on this day, of all days.

Ryan took Sage to the Green Dragon Restaurant for their first date. She had heard about the restaurant but had never eaten there before.

"This is a really nice place," she said, her eyes bouncing around a dining room draped in rich burgundy and gold tones. The green foliage added to the exotic ambience.

"I'm glad you like it," he responded. "I heard about this place back in New York. It was on my list to try it whenever the opportunity presented itself."

Ryan couldn't seem to take his eyes off her and the

thought pleased Sage. She had picked out the dress she was wearing with him in mind.

Sage was ready to throw caution to the wind where he was concerned. She knew that he was attracted to her, but Ryan had been nothing but a perfect gentleman where she was concerned.

Their waiter brought out the food, arranging it on the table.

They made small talk while they ate.

Sage loved the way Ryan's kissable lips parted when he laughed that deep, throaty laugh. He was a very handsome and sexy man—a striking contrast to when she met him for the first time.

At the end of the evening, Ryan escorted her up to her place.

Sage unlocked her door and then turned around to face Ryan. He leaned over and kissed her. "I really enjoyed our first date."

She resisted the urge to touch the place where his lips had been. Her heart was racing, and Sage could feel her blood rushing through her veins.

She glanced up at Ryan, who said, "I didn't offend you just now, did I?"

"No, you didn't," she answered quickly. Sage's heart fluttered wildly in her chest. His nearness sent a shiver of wanting through her. "Not at all."

Ryan pulled Sage into his arms, his mouth covering hers hungrily.

She returned his kiss with a hunger that belied her outward calm. Burying her face in his neck, Sage breathed a kiss there.

"You have no idea how long I've wanted to kiss you," Ryan confessed.

"Probably as many times as I've wanted you to kiss me."

"Sage, I don't know where this is going, but I do know that I care about you."

"We don't have to try and figure this out tonight, Ryan. We like each other. Let's just leave it at that for now."

"I'm not a womanizer. I want you to know that."

She smiled. "That's nice to hear. I'm not in the mood for drama."

"I want to see where this goes, Sage. But I can't help but wonder how your family is going to feel about this."

"I feel the same way," she responded. "And you don't have to worry about my family. I can handle them."

They made plans to have dinner at her place the following evening.

Ryan gathered her into his arms and held her snugly. "This feels good, holding you like this."

Sage's skin tingled where he touched her. Standing on tiptoe, she touched her lips to his. She could not resist just one more kiss before sending him away. Tomorrow was a busy day for her, and she did not want to stay up too late. It was already after ten o'clock.

Sage showered and dressed for bed.

She had truly enjoyed herself with Ryan during dinner.

Despite all that he had been through, he was still able to have a wonderful sense of humor. He possessed such a warm loving spirit, and he always seemed to wear a smile.

Sage settled down in her bed, a smile tugging at her lips.

She was beginning to develop real feelings for Ryan. The silent declaration did not really surprise Sage. She only hoped that her family would understand and trust her to make the right choices for her life.

Ryan has proven to be everything she thought him to be; surely her family would give their relationship a chance.

Sage was still on Ryan's mind when he arrived at his room. Sage had a wonderful sense of humor. He had enjoyed the evening with her. Not only was she beautiful but she was intelligent and caring, as well. The more he learned about her, the more he wanted to know about her. An undeniable magnetism was building between them, forcing him to acknowledge the truth.

I'm falling in love with Sage Alexander, and I haven't been completely honest with her.

It had been a mistake to get this close to her, but it was too late now. There really wasn't any turning back. Ryan was not sure he could turn away from Sage at this point, even if he wanted to do so. He could no longer fight temptation.

Ryan vowed to tell Sage everything when the time was right. Could a relationship work between them once she knew the truth? Ryan didn't have the answer to that, but he hoped that they would be able to work through whatever issues would arise out of his confession.

He thought about calling Sage just so that her voice was the last thing he heard before he went to sleep, but he resisted the urge.

Ryan felt heat radiating from his loins and shifted in his seat on the edge of the bed. He was going to have to take a cold shower tonight. It was a struggle to keep his desire for Sage under control.

Groaning, he removed his shoes and socks. Ryan stood up and took off his clothes. He padded barefoot and nude into the bathroom.

He emerged ten minutes later in a fluffy robe. His body still ached for Sage's touch, but Ryan forced the thoughts out of his mind by turning his thoughts to the article he had to write.

Ryan sat down at the desk and removed his iPad and wireless keyboard from the backpack that had clearly seen better days. He planned to purchase a new one soon, but for now, he had to keep his tablet concealed. Ryan had no way of explaining how he could afford one of those in his present condition.

He worked until well past midnight.

His article was going in a different direction from the way he had planned it initially. Ryan decided to go with the flow. He trusted his creative instincts and had relied on them to guide him his entire career.

Sage floated through Ryan's mind.

He closed his eyes, savoring the vision of her beauty.

Ryan picked up one of the pillows and put it to his face, muffling his groan. It was going to be a very long night.

Sage could not fathom how her family was going to react when they found out that she had strong feelings for Ryan.

It did not matter what they thought, she kept telling

herself. She was a grown woman, she was smart…she had thought long and hard about a potential relationship with Ryan. She had no doubts where he was concerned.

She and Meredith had a meeting to attend at the corporate offices, so they prepared to leave.

They ran into Ryan in the lobby area.

Sage allowed her eyes to linger, appreciating the strong lines of his well-formed cheeks and jaw. However, it was those penetrating eyes of his that arrested her—intelligent eyes that seemed to peer through to her very soul.

"Good morning, ladies," he said.

Sage and Meredith returned the greeting in unison.

"He seems like a nice man," Meredith commented as they headed out to the car. Sage had called and requested that the valet deliver it to the front of the hotel.

"Ryan is very nice."

"You two are becoming close friends, I see."

Sage glanced over at Meredith. "Is there a question somewhere in there?"

They walked out of the hotel.

Once they were inside the car, Meredith said, "I apologize if I came off as being nosy. I actually think you two make a wonderful couple."

"Meredith, you seem to know more about my life. Tell me about you. Are you seeing someone?"

She smiled. "I have a boyfriend, and we're actually talking about getting married. The only thing is that he is still in law school. He doesn't want to get married until after he graduates."

"When will he be finished with school?"

"In another year."

Sage glanced over at her cousin. "But you don't want to wait that long?"

"No, I don't. Dale and I have been together since my junior year in high school. All of my friends are getting married and…well, they haven't been with their boyfriends as long as I have been with Dale."

"Meredith, you're still young. You don't have to rush into a marriage because your friends are getting married."

"I know," she said. "Sage, I feel that I'm ready to settle down. Dating is fine, but I want to come home to Dale in the evenings and wake up next to him in the mornings."

Sage understood exactly how Meredith felt. "I'll be thirty in a couple of months. I feel the same way that you do…only I haven't met the man of my dreams yet."

"Are you sure?"

She gave Meredith a sidelong glance. "What are you talking about?"

"Ryan Manning. He has feelings for you from the way you look at him. I know that you care for him, as well."

"I do," she confirmed.

"You do know that once your relationship gets out, it will probably be all over the tabloids."

"I'm sure your brother will see to that," Sage uttered. As soon as the words left her mouth, she regretted them. "Meredith, I'm sorry. I really shouldn't have said that to you."

"It's okay, Sage. I know what Harold tried to do to you all. The truth is that he still has not gotten used to the idea that Uncle Robert had a son. I think he felt betrayed in some way."

"That's fine—I don't know how I would feel in his shoes, but to attack my family… We had nothing to do with the choices Robert DePaul made. We had no idea that we were even related to the man."

"We acted selfishly, Sage," Meredith stated. "We all did. I'm really sorry for my part in it. I hope that we can build a close relationship. I like you."

"We're talking about boys, so I would say that we are well on our way, don't you think?"

Grinning, Meredith nodded.

Chapter 11

Although the grand opening of Le Magnifique was a week away, Ryan performed a quick inventory to make sure the restaurant kitchen had a fully stocked pantry.

When he started his job, some of the kitchen staff seemed opposed to the idea that the Alexander family would plant a man who had been homeless in the position of manager, but he soon earned their respect when it became clear that he was knowledgeable when it came to cooking and running the restaurant.

According to the rumor mill, he was a former restaurant owner who had fallen down on his luck and lost everything. Ryan didn't bother to deny or confirm the rumor.

He had spoken to Sage earlier about a friend needing a job after learning that there were some openings at the hotel. After their conversation, he called Paige and told her to come prepared for an interview.

Ryan thought she would be perfect for the hotel nanny position. She would be able to bring Cassie to work with her as the hotel had a day-care facility for its employees.

He left his assistant manager in charge and left to meet Paige in the lobby area.

Ryan nodded in approval when he saw her. Paige had pulled her hair back into a neat ponytail. She wore a simple navy dress with a gold chain draped around her neck. On her feet, she wore a pair of gold-and-navy-colored strappy sandals with a three-inch heel.

It was probably one of the few pieces of clothing she still owned. She had told Ryan that someone had stolen her suitcase while she was sleeping her first night at the shelter.

"I'm so nervous," Paige told Ryan.

"Just be yourself," he suggested. "I'm sure you'll get the job. You've worked at a day care before, so you have experience with a variety of children—not to mention that you're also a mother.

"I'll watch Cassie for you, so you don't have to worry about anything."

"Are you sure about this?" Paige asked. "I don't want to get you in any trouble."

"You're not going to get me in any trouble," Ryan responded. "I don't have to go back to work for another hour. I took the afternoon off so that I could watch Cassie for you while you have your interview." He loved children, but his ex-wife had never wanted any—another issue in their marriage that they could not overcome.

"You are probably the nicest person I've ever met, Ryan. Thank you so much for everything."

Ryan took Cassie out of her arms. "You're welcome,

Paige. When I was eight, my parents died in a fire. My next-door neighbors had five children of their own, but they took my brother and me in and raised us. They never once treated us as if we didn't belong. They were good parents."

"Wow," Paige murmured.

"It wasn't that my parents were close to them or anything, but what family I had didn't want to take on an extra burden. I used to play with their children, and they didn't want me getting lost in the foster care system. They adopted me."

"So you always pay it forward, don't you?"

He smiled. "I've been blessed, and it's only right that I be a blessing to others. This is why we were created... well, and to praise God."

"You're a Christian."

"I prefer to say that I am a believer," Ryan responded. He had come to see that many who called themselves Christian did not live as the claim they often made. As he considered this, he felt a thread of guilt snake down his spine. Although he was gathering research for a story, the reality was that he had deceived all of them, including Paige.

Ryan hoped they would all understand once the truth came out. He was just doing his job.

Sage waited for Ryan and his friend in her office.

While she waited for them to arrive, Sage made a mental note to have a place for the man to clean up before the meeting in an attempt to preserve what little dignity he had left. She left her office to make the necessary arrangements but slowed her steps when Ryan stepped off the elevator with his friend.

Sage struggled to hide her initial shock of seeing Ryan with a petite young female carrying a baby girl.

The baby is biracial. Is the child related to Ryan in some way?

Pushing the question to the back of her mind, Sage quickly recovered and said, "Please, have a seat."

Ryan made the introductions. "This is my *friend* Paige Baker."

Smiling, Sage rose to her feet and said, "It's very nice to meet you." She silently noted that he seemed to stress the word *friend* when he referred to Paige, but she could not dismiss the loving way he cradled the little girl close to his chest.

There is definitely a connection between Paige, the baby and Ryan.

A wave of sadness flowed through her, but she decided to ignore it. Sage didn't fully understand why she felt the jealousy that coursed through her, but she was determined to push past her secret feelings to help Ryan and his family.

"I told Paige about the nanny position," Ryan stated.

"I'm really interested in applying," Paige interjected. "I have experience in child care. I've been babysitting others' kids since I was thirteen years old. I have first-aid training and CPR certification, and I can provide references."

"I'm sold," Sage said with a smile. "I'll make a call to Joan and let her know that you are on your way up to the personnel department. She's the hiring manager for that position."

"Thank you so much, Ms. Alexander. I really appreciate your help."

"We have a day care for the hotel staff, so this job will allow you to keep your daughter nearby while you work."

Paige's eyes fill with tears. "Oh, my goodness, this just sounds too good to be true. If I get the job, I can find somewhere to live."

"The job also comes with a room here in the staff quarters. Working as a hotel nanny requires that you be on-site," Sage explained as she eyed Ryan. "We can have a crib put in there if that will help."

He glanced over at Paige, who nodded. "I appreciate all of your help, Ms. Alexander. I promise you that I will work very hard for you if given the chance."

"I have a very good feeling about you, Paige."

Sage could feel Ryan's eyes on her. She was careful to keep her face a blank canvas. She did not want him to have any idea how tumultuous her emotions were at this point. Sage silently chided herself for envying Ryan's relationship with Paige—whatever it may be.

If he truly is that child's father, can I handle this? she thought.

Sage decided that she needed a night on the town. She picked up the telephone and called Meredith.

"Hey, girl," Sage said when her cousin answered the telephone.

"Do you have any plans for tonight?" she asked Meredith.

"No, I don't. Dale has to work on a paper, so I'll be home tonight alone and bored. What's up?"

"I was thinking about going out to a movie. It's been a while since I've been out to anything that isn't business related."

Meredith gave a short sigh. "I know the feeling. A movie sounds really wonderful because nothing good is on television these days."

Sage smiled. "Great. Let's plan to grab something to eat after work, and then we'll catch a movie."

They talked for a few minutes more before hanging up.

The image of him with that baby haunted Sage's thoughts. She desperately wanted to know exactly what Ryan's relationship with Paige was. She did not want to deal with any baby-mama drama.

Ryan was thrilled for Paige.

All the paperwork was done, and pending the results of her background check, the job was hers.

Cassie was sleeping in his arms. She was getting bigger and she seemed heavier, which meant she was growing. Ryan had fallen in love with the little girl and felt protective of her. Paige teased him about being Cassie's uncle. In fact, when talking to the baby, she always referred to him as Uncle Ryan.

He didn't mind. His brother had two children whom Ryan adored. He still held out hope that he would one day remarry and have a family. His ex-wife had deliberately misled him into believing that they would have children. Their marriage was shaky, but once he found the birth control pills she kept hidden under the mattress it was over. They had supposedly been trying for a baby.

The baby stirred in his arms. Smiling, he cradled her closer.

Ryan caught sight of Sage and rushed over to speak with her. "I wanted to thank you personally for what you did for Paige."

"I should be thanking you," she responded. "She comes with excellent references, I'm told."

"She's been through a lot and…"

Sage cut him off. "I'm sorry, but I have to get to a meeting. I'm looking forward to getting to know Paige."

Ryan was a little confused by her actions. She had always been so warm and friendly. Sage did say that she had a meeting to attend, but deep down he felt that there was something more going on.

He recalled the look of surprise that Sage wore when she saw Paige and the baby. At that time, Ryan thought that it was because of the baby, but now another thought occurred to him: Sage was jealous.

The idea brought a smile to his lips. She had nothing to worry about where Paige was concerned. He viewed the young woman as he would a sibling. Paige considered Ryan a big brother, as well.

He would explain the relationship the moment he saw Sage again. He did not want that sort of misunderstanding lingering as they were building the foundation of a relationship.

Chapter 12

Meredith strode into the office a few minutes after Sage arrived.

"I had a great time with you last night," she said. "I really hope that we can do something like that on a regular basis."

Sage smiled at her cousin, pleased with the way their relationship was progressing. Sage discovered that she and Meredith had a lot in common. "We can do it any time you want, Meredith. I had a good time, as well."

They had dinner together and then went to see a movie. She and Meredith had even shared a tub of popcorn with extra butter. Sage had fully enjoyed spending time with her cousin.

Sage's telephone rang.

She answered on the second ring. "This is Sage Alexander."

"This is Ryan Manning."

She glanced over at Meredith. "Hey…"

"I called you last night, but I guess you were out," Ryan told her. "I wanted to see if we could talk."

"I had a girl's night out with Meredith. Ryan, is something wrong?" Sage wanted to know.

"No."

"What do you want to talk about?" she asked him.

"I wanted to explain my relationship with Paige. I owe you that much. Can we meet at your place to talk at some point today?"

"How about three o'clock?" Sage suggested.

She tried to maintain her focus on her tasks, but it was difficult. Sage kept trying to figure out what he would tell her.

When the clock struck two-thirty, Sage told her assistant that she would be in her penthouse for the rest of the day.

There was no sign of Ryan when she stepped off the elevator. Sage unlocked her door and went inside.

Sage paced back and forth across her hardwood floor, her stomach full of nervous energy. Ryan had called earlier and asked to meet her at her penthouse. He said that he needed to explain his relationship with Paige.

She had no idea what he was going to tell her. However, it had to be serious because he wanted to meet in private.

He is going to tell me that he is the father of that baby.

It was torture waiting for Ryan to arrive. Sage just wanted to get it over and done with.

There was a loud knock on the door, which startled her.

Sage stepped aside so that Ryan could enter. He had stopped to pick up some food for them.

They did not talk much while they ate.

Sage had never known Ryan to be so quiet. Every now and then Sage would catch him watching her. It was as if he were photographing her with his eyes. She could not help but wonder if this would be the last time they would be together like this.

This was a bad sign, she thought. In the past, they had had stimulating conversations over meals.

Finally, Sage could not take it anymore. She pushed her plate away and said, "Ryan, what did you come here to talk about? I'd rather we get that out of the way."

"Sage, I know that you must have some questions regarding my relationship with Paige."

She did not respond. Sage wanted to hear him out first.

"Paige and I are only friends. She sees me like a big brother. I met her on the streets. She's going through something, and with a baby... I just thought that she would be able to find a job here at the hotel. I only wanted to help her."

She wiped her mouth on the edge of her napkin before saying, "So the baby is not yours?"

"No, she's not. Cassie's father walked out on them shortly after she was born."

"I admit that I jumped to conclusions," she confessed. "I knew that you said you were from New York and had no family out here. I assumed that you didn't really have many friends."

"Sage, tell me something...were you jealous?"

"Why would you ask me that?" she asked, stalling.

He grinned. "You're not going to answer my question, are you?"

She shook her head. "If you want to know the truth… I'm tired of talking. There are more important things we could be doing."

Ryan understood the meaning behind her words. He pulled her into his arms, kissing her.

Sage responded hungrily.

"You never have to worry about me and another woman, Sage." Ryan's gaze was riveted on her face. "I love you, Sage."

She opened her mouth to speak, but no words came out.

When she found her voice, she murmured, "Please tell me that I didn't hear you wrong. Can you say it again, please?"

Ryan smiled. "I love you."

Ryan wrapped his arms around her. "This feels so right to me," he whispered. "I tried to fight my feelings, but I just couldn't give you up. I don't expect for you to declare your love or anyth—"

Sage cut him off by placing her hand over his mouth. "I love you, too, Ryan."

Reclaiming her lips, Ryan crushed her to him. Her calm was shattered with the hunger of his kisses.

Sage took Ryan by the hand and led him into her bedroom.

He met her heated gaze. "Are you sure?"

Their eyes locked as their breathing came in unison.

She nodded. "I'm ready to take our relationship to the next level."

Sage walked over to the bedroom door, closing it shut.

She was filled with an inner excitement in anticipation of what they were about to share.

Later that evening, Ryan and Sage stood on the balcony of her unit, admiring the beauty of her surroundings. She pulled the folds of her sweater together.

"Cold?"

"It's a little breezy out here, but I'm fine," she told Ryan. "I love to come out here and just sit. The view is really beautiful, especially at night. It's very romantic."

Ryan agreed.

"So you consider this romantic?" Ryan teased, placing an arm around her. "Standing out here on the balcony in the moonlight?"

Sage gave him a playful slap on the arm. "Yeah, I do." She savored the sultry sounds of Ryan's laughter. "Especially after making love." She rubbed her arms through the sweater, trying to ward off the goose bumps from the brisk air.

They went back inside the penthouse.

Sage and Ryan sat down on the sofa in the living room.

"Do you have any regrets about what we did?" Ryan asked as he played with a curling tendril of her hair.

Sage shook her head no. "None at all. How about you?"

"No regrets," he responded.

Ryan kissed her.

His kiss was slow and thoughtful, and it sent spirals of desire racing through Sage.

"I am a blessed man to have found you, Sage."

She smiled, touched by his words.

Ryan could hardly wait for everything to be out in the open. Only then would he be able to lift the weight of the world off his shoulders. He wanted to be able to confide in her, share his real life with Sage.

She snuggled against him. "Why are you so quiet?"

"I was thinking about you," he responded. "I have never loved anyone as much as I love you, Sage. There's so much I want to say to you, but it will have to wait until the time is right."

"Ryan, you can tell me anything."

He searched her face. Ryan could tell that she was sincere and meant every word, but she had no idea what he was keeping from her.

The summer months passed quickly with Sage and Ryan spending a lot of time together when they were not working.

Ari and Natasha's wedding was just weeks away. Sage was glad because Ari was so busy that he had no time to lecture her about dating Ryan. He and Blaze made it known that they were not thrilled about her relationship with Ryan; however, her mother and father decided to trust her choice.

The restaurant had had a successful grand opening, and food critics raved about the food. Ryan was responsible for its success.

Sage was very proud of Ryan and his hard work. He was proving to be a man she could trust with her entire being.

She glanced at the clock.

She needed to begin preparing dinner. Ryan was coming by after work, and she'd promised him a home-cooked meal. They were similar in that they both preferred to eat at home over restaurant food.

He arrived promptly at seven.

Sage threw open the door and stepped aside to let Ryan enter the penthouse. Leaning into him, Sage welcomed his warm embrace.

"I'm so glad to see you, sweetheart," he murmured in her hair. "I want you to know that it was hard to get my work done, because you were on my mind all day long."

Sage wrapped her arms around him, and replied, "It was the same for me. At one point, I really thought this day would never end."

Ryan laughed. "I know what you mean. I kept thinking that there had to be something wrong with my watch."

Sage gestured toward the love seat and said, "Give me a few minutes to set everything up, and then we can eat."

"Take your time, sweetheart. We have all evening."

Ten minutes later, Sage led Ryan into the dining room.

He eyed the beautifully decorated table. Vibrant flames flickered from the gold-colored candles, casting a soft glow on the succulent display of lobster, coleslaw, garlic bread and steaming asparagus. "Everything looks delicious."

"Thank you." Sage sat down in the chair Ryan pulled out for her. He eased into a chair facing her.

After giving thanks, they dug into their food.

Ryan appeared to be thoroughly enjoying the meal, which thrilled Sage. She considered him a much better cook than she was, so Sage only cooked the types of foods she prepared well.

After dinner, Ryan helped her with the cleanup, which was definitely a first for her. None of the men she had dated in the past ever came into the kitchen unless it was to get something to eat or drink.

Later, curled up on the sofa together, Ryan acknowledged, "The lobster was excellent. You did a wonderful job, sweetheart."

Sage never tired of looking at him. His brown eyes were lit up from within with a golden glow. She reached over to pinch him.

"What was that for?" he asked.

"I just needed to know if you are for real."

Ryan threw back his head and laughed.

"I'm serious, Ryan," Sage said. "I have to be real with you. There are times when you seem almost too good to be true."

"Sweetheart, I'm for real," Ryan responded. "To tell the truth, I was feeling the same way about you, Sage. I mean, I have never met a woman that I considered perfect for me—not like you are."

"No one has ever treated me the way you do. It's kind of foreign. Do you know what I mean?"

"I do," he responded. "Sage, I'm not going to change if that's what you're worried about. I've been heartbroken before, and it's not something that I want to inflict on someone else. The truth is that I tried to fight my feelings for you. I wanted to keep a professional distance, but my heart would not let me." Ryan gazed into her eyes. "Honey, I want you to know that I would never intentionally cause you pain."

"I believe you," Sage responded. Moving closer, she laid her head on his chest.

Together, they watched television.

Three hours later, Ryan gently sat Sage up and rose to his feet. "I guess I'd better get going. We both have to work tomorrow."

Sage did not want him to leave.

Sage stood up, too. She still ached for his touch so much, and her feelings for him were intensifying, wrapping around her like a warm blanket. Her emotions melted her resolve. "Don't leave. I want you to stay with me tonight."

"Are you sure about this?" Ryan wanted to know. They had been very careful to keep their relationship as quiet as possible. Neither one of them wanted the media following their romance.

His steady gaze bore in her in silent expectation.

In response, Sage led him by the hand to her bedroom.

Standing in the middle of the floor, they undressed each other in silence.

Ryan held her in his arms, his eyes making passionate love to her with his gaze. Taking in his powerful presence, she asked, "What is it?"

"I knew you were special from the first time I ever saw you. You looked liked an angel to me, and when you put that money in my hands, I was convinced. I love you, angel."

Sage was moved by his words. "I feel the same way about you."

She watched the play of emotions on his face.

Ryan swept her, weightless, into his arms and carried her to the bed. He crawled in behind her after placing her in the middle of the bed.

Sage could feel his uneven breathing on her cheek as he held her close. The touch of Ryan's hand was almost unbearable in its tenderness. His mouth covered hers hungrily, leaving her mouth burning with fire.

The touch of her lips on his sent a shock wave through his entire body with a savage intensity. Ryan planted kisses on her shoulders, neck and face. As he roused her passion, his own need grew stronger.

Passion pounded the blood through her heart, chest and head, causing Sage to breathe in deep soul-drenching drafts.

She had never been as happily in love as she was in this moment in time, and she did not want it to end.

Chapter 13

"I can't thank you enough for this second chance, Ms. Alexander."

"It's just Sage," she interjected. "Paige, we are glad to have you working here. You're doing a fantastic job from what I hear."

She smiled. "I'm getting a lot of referrals."

"That's wonderful."

Sage had heard from Ryan that Paige was going out with Keith, the assistant manager at Le Magnifique.

Keith was a sweetheart and had been a model employee. Ari hired him right out of college, placing him in the management training program. Sage was genuinely happy for Paige. The young woman was a devoted mother and a hard worker; she deserved to have some downtime and a social life.

"I offered to babysit Cassie while they're on their date," he told her.

"Can I keep you company?"

Ryan smiled. "I was hoping that you would say that."

"Bring her up to my place," Sage suggested.

He kissed her. "I can't wait."

"Oh, my parents invited us to the house for the weekend. I guess it's time for you to have that sit-down with them."

He grinned. "I'm okay with that."

Sage folded her arms across her chest. "Really? So, you're not just a little bit afraid of my father?"

Ryan shook his head. "I have a lot of respect for Malcolm, but I do not fear him."

"He's fair," she stated.

"You can't ask for any more than that."

Sage agreed.

Later that evening, she and Ryan sat in the middle of the floor, playing with Cassie.

"She's so cute," Sage murmured. "And she's getting so big."

Ryan agreed.

Sage loved spending time with Cassie. She was a good baby and always had a smile on her face. Paige was wonderful with children and obviously a good mother. Despite her time on the streets, she had not let it embitter her. Like her daughter, she wore a smile most of the time. She and Ryan were close, but their relationship was strictly a platonic one. Anyone seeing the two of them together would eventually come to the same conclusion.

"I have a confession to make."

He glanced over at Sage. "What is it, sweetheart?"

"When you brought Paige to my office that first

time, I thought that maybe she was your ex-girlfriend. I thought Cassie was your little girl."

"So you *were* jealous," Ryan stated with a grin.

Sage was about to deny it but changed her mind. "Okay, I was just a little jealous. I jumped to the wrong conclusion when I saw you with Cassie. It's clear that this little girl has you wrapped around her tiny little finger."

Ryan smiled. "There is a not-so-little girl who also has me wrapped around her little finger."

She leaned over and kissed him.

"You don't talk much about your past relationships," Sage stated. "Why is that?"

Ryan shrugged. "Because it is a part of my past, and I tend to try to focus on the present and my future."

"Sometimes it is good to look back and learn from past mistakes."

He agreed. "It's okay to do that, but what ends up happening is that most people cannot seem to come to grips with their past. They do not learn from it or they don't know how to move forward."

Cassie reached for her rattle.

Sage picked it up and held it out to the baby. "Is this what you want?"

"Do you want children someday?" he asked, surprising her.

Sage met his gaze. "Yeah. I'd like to have at least two. What about you?"

"I want to be a father when the time is right."

She laughed. "Is there ever really a right time?"

He shrugged. "I don't know. I suppose when that desire becomes a reality that it will be the right time."

* * *

Sage gave Cassie a bath.

"You are such a darling," she murmured as the baby splashed in her tub. "I hope to bathe my little girl or baby boy like this one day."

She was not aware of Ryan's presence until she turned around. "What are you doing in here?" she asked. "This little lady needs her privacy, don't you?"

"I love watching you with her," he said.

Sage wondered if he had heard her talking about wanting a baby. She did not want him to think that she was desperate to have a child, because she was not. Besides, a marriage had to happen first. She was not interested in having children without a husband. Two of her friends back home had gotten pregnant—one in high school and the other in college. Both women were still single and struggling to raise their children without support from the fathers. Sage had learned from their mistakes.

Paige and Keith came to the penthouse around ten.

They sat down with Ryan and Sage to talk for a few minutes before taking Cassie with them to Paige's room.

Sage cuddled up with Ryan on the sofa. She had no idea whether her relationship with him would lead to marriage, but a part of her believed she would spend the rest of her life with Ryan.

Ryan watched Sage as she slept.

He wanted so much to share the part of him that he kept secret from her. Ryan wanted to give all of himself over to Sage; he loved her that much. Thinking about what had transpired earlier, he watched the rise and fall of her chest as Sage slept. She made him feel loved in the way that she touched him, kissed him and held him in her arms.

He closed his eyes, seeking sleep, but images from his past resurfaced, forcing him to stay wide-awake. Ryan shook his head, trying to shake the turbulent thoughts away.

Sage turned on her side. She moaned softly but never opened her eyes.

Ryan really hated the idea of keeping parts of his life from her. There should never be secrets between two people who were in love. However, he also believed that most couples did not share every single aspect of their lives with each other.

Early the next morning, they climbed out of bed and went to the gym to work out. Ryan had never been on a health kick, but he enjoyed working out with Sage. They started out by stretching and then headed to the treadmill.

They ended their workout by lifting weights. Sage's body was well toned, and Ryan learned that this was the way she kept her weight down.

"I love to eat, so I have to work out at least four days a week," she had told him when they first started working out together.

Just as they were about to leave the gym, Ari walked in.

"You two leaving?" he asked.

Sage nodded. "I have a meeting in less than an hour."

Ari and Ryan discussed the restaurant for a brief moment.

"I guess he's trying," Sage whispered as they left the

gym. "Ari has always been very protective of all of us. I guess he feels that he has to because he is the eldest. He has nothing to worry about from you, though."

Ryan did not respond.

When they neared the private elevator, Sage said, "I need to get going. I'll see you for lunch."

They kissed.

Sage gave him a smile and then stepped onto the elevator.

He had not really considered that it wasn't just Sage he had to worry about once the truth came out. Ryan would have to deal with her entire family.

Harold sat down at the table where Meredith was having breakfast. She looked up from her newspaper. "What are you doing here? Don't you have a hotel of your own to run?"

"Now you are beginning to sound like the Alexanders."

"You haven't answered my question."

"I have heard some potentially damaging news. There's talk that Sage is dating some man she found on the streets. Is this true?"

"What business is it of yours?" Meredith asked. "Harold, why are you so consumed with Malcolm and his family? You know, some might consider you a stalker of sorts."

He dismissed her words with a slight wave of his hand. "I knew that your working with Sage was going to be trouble."

"Actually, it's been quite enlightening," she countered. "She and I are becoming great friends."

Harold frowned. "You just be careful. They are not to be trusted."

She gave him a wry smile. "They say the same thing about you."

"Where is your sense of loyalty?" he challenged. "You and I...we are brother and sister. How dare you choose them over your own flesh and blood."

"I'm not going to allow you to put me in the middle of this mess you created. I like the Alexanders, and I'll have no part in any of your schemes to get back at them for some imagined wrong."

His mouth twisted in anger. "I hope one day you will realize that you chose the wrong side, Meredith."

"And I hope you'll come to realize that there is really only one side. We are all a part of the DePaul family. We should stick together and not be divided. Malcolm and his family has done nothing to warrant the attacks you've sent their way." Meredith sent her brother an angry glare. "You have no problem going after anyone in that family. It is not their fault for what happened. If you want to be angry at someone then be angry at Uncle Robert. He is the one responsible for all that's transpired."

She rose to her feet. "I need to get to the office."

"Meredith..."

She shook her head. "I'm done with this conversation, Harold. You really need to find a way to deal with your anger issues. Perhaps you should seek therapy."

Sage and Ryan spent the weekend on Catalina Island, a popular destination located about twenty-two miles southwest of Los Angeles.

They both wanted some time away from the hotel and Beverly Hills.

"I'm so glad we decided to get away," Sage said as they walked out of their suite in the cozy bed-and-breakfast inn. As they descended the stairs, she said, "I could stay here forever."

Ryan felt the same way. Although he never said anything to Sage, Ryan felt as if his every move was under scrutiny at the hotel. "I can see why you love coming over here. The island is beautiful."

Sage nodded. "This is my second time coming here. The first time was with my mother and sister. We decided to come here so that the men could bond."

As soon as they stepped outside, Sage beheld her surroundings. It was so amazing how the fall season just seemed to wash the island in brilliant waves of color. Immersed in the sea of heavenly hues as people milled around them, Ryan and Sage strolled casually along the sidewalks, pausing every now and then to peruse items in the local shops.

"I really needed this little getaway. It seems that I cannot keep my desk clear. We have sold almost all of the vacant residences, and a previously occupied one will be for sale soon. The owners want us to list it."

Ryan held her hand and kept her close to him at all times, which thrilled Sage. No man had ever made her feel so special.

"What are you thinking about?" Ryan asked, intruding on her thoughts.

"I was just thinking that no man I've ever dated has made me feel the way you do. You treat me like a queen."

"That's because you are a queen to me," Ryan interjected. "A woman who is as beautiful on the inside as she is on the outside deserves to be treated like royalty. I love and appreciate your friendship, your love and your honesty."

Sage took his hand in hers. "Please don't place me on a pedestal, Ryan. I'm not perfect. I have flaws—quite a few actually."

He met her gaze. "You are perfect in every way to me."

Chapter 14

"You and my sister are getting really close," Ari stated when he strolled into Ryan's office. "I've been busy with wedding plans, but I want to talk to you. Do you have a minute?"

Ryan motioned for Ari to take a seat.

"I'm in love with your sister," he stated. "Sage loves me in return."

"She had made that clear to all of us," Ari responded.

"Are you concerned that my intentions toward your sister are not pure?"

"I'm sure you would be just as concerned if the roles were reversed."

Ryan had to admit that Ari was right. He would try to protect his sister, if he had one. "You're right."

"I don't want you to think that I have anything against you, Ryan. It's just that I love my sister, and I don't like seeing her get hurt."

"I will never intentionally hurt Sage. Ari, I give you my word."

"Great," Ari responded as he rose to his feet. "Sage is very caring, and loyalty is extremely important to her. I hope you will keep that in mind."

Ari left the office.

Ryan swallowed hard. He was almost done with his research. For a brief moment, he considered not going through with the articles, but the subject matter was something he cared about deeply. He couldn't turn back now.

He didn't want to lose Sage either.

Ryan picked up the phone and dialed her office extension.

"This is Sage Alexander," she announced.

"Hello, beautiful."

"Ryan, hey…"

"Can you come to my office?" Ryan asked.

"Sure. I'll be there in a few minutes. I need to make a quick phone call first."

While he waited, Ryan played what he was going to say in his head. He prayed the right words would come out of his mouth.

But mostly he prayed that he would not lose Sage. He hoped that in time she would be able to forgive him. Ryan was not prepared to have this conversation, but it could not wait any longer. He had to tell her everything today.

Ryan leaned back in his chair. "Please let this turn out okay," he whispered to the empty room.

Sage had no idea why Ryan wanted to see her, but it did not really matter. She always looked forward to spending time with him.

She entered his office wearing a smile. "What's up, Ryan?"

He gestured for her to take a seat on the sofa.

Ryan pushed away from his desk and stood up. He walked across the carpet to join her.

Sage planted a kiss on his lips.

She noted a glimmer of apprehension in his eyes. "Is something wrong?"

"There's something I have to tell you."

"Honey, what is it?" she asked, her voice filled with concern.

"I love you so much."

Sage smiled. "I love you, too. You are the first man I have ever met that I can say that I trust with my life. I wish there were more men in this world like you."

"I would do anything to keep you safe. I hope you know that, Sage."

She reached over and touched Ryan's face. "I believe you, and I would do the same for you."

They shared a kiss.

"One of the things I love most about you is your honesty. Total honesty is a rare quality in a person, but I've found it in you, Ryan. I love that we have no secrets between us. I don't think I could deal with someone who is unable to be truthful with me, especially about the little things."

Ryan was silent.

"I'm not putting you on a pedestal," Sage said with a smile. "I'm just speaking the truth about you."

"I hope that I can one day prove to be worthy of your love, Sage."

"Honey, you already have," she assured him. "I feel

so close to you, Ryan. I trust you so completely. It's freeing to know that you can feel that way about a person."

She glanced at her watch. "Oh, I have to get going, but what did you want to tell me?"

"That I love you with all my heart."

Sage smiled at him. "Aww...honey. I never tire of hearing you say that."

"Then I won't stop saying it," Ryan promised. "I won't let a day go by without my telling you how much you mean to me."

Sage savored the feel of Ryan's lips on hers.

On the way back to her office, it struck her that Ryan hadn't really seemed like himself. Sage paused a moment before opening the door and considered going back to see him, but she really did not have time. She would catch up with him later.

Sage ran into Franklin and his daughter Tammie in the elevator.

"Where have you two been?" she asked. "I haven't seen either one of you in a while."

"Dad took me to Italy," Tammie announced. "It was a birthday present to me."

"I wanted to do something special to make up for all of the birthdays I missed when she was growing up."

Sage broke into a grin. "I think that's wonderful. It's a great birthday present. How are things working out with Drayden as your boss? You can always come work here at the hotel if he's not treating you right."

"Drayden is wonderful," Tammie said. "I've learned a lot from him. He actually thinks I should sit for the CPA exam."

Franklin agreed. "I've been telling her that I think

she's already invested so much into her education that she might as well go for it all."

"If they haven't convinced you already, then let me throw in my vote," Sage said. "Tammie, if this is something you want to do then do it. Life is short."

She got off the elevator when the door opened.

Sage thought about Ryan and smiled. He was absolutely perfect as far as she was concerned. Sure, he had some flaws, but she had yet to uncover any. He was definitely a dream come true.

"What's got you in such a happy mood?" Ryan asked her the next morning over breakfast.

Sage flashed him a grin and said, "I was thinking about last night and how beautiful it was being with you. We're really good together, but it's not just about the sex." Her eyes met his intense gaze. "Ryan, I have so much to be thankful for."

Sitting down beside her at the dining room table, Ryan smiled. "I'm just glad you're happy.

"You're not hungry?" he asked, pointing to her plate.

Sage patted him lovingly on the back, and said, "While you're eating, I'm going to go up and take my shower."

Chewing, Ryan nodded.

Sage hummed as she made her way to the bathroom.

While she showered, Sage reflected upon her favorite pastime of late—Ari and Natasha's upcoming wedding, which was less than two weeks away.

She and her mother were helping Natasha choose the wedding favors and the flowers. She enjoyed helping out, but she could not wait to take some time to relax after her brother's marriage.

While Ryan went to work in the restaurant, Sage met Meredith and Paige in the spa for a day of pampering.

"I so needed this," Sage murmured as she was getting a massage.

"I've never experienced anything like this," Paige said. "Thanks so much for inviting me."

"We girls work hard, so we have to stick together," Meredith interjected. "I say we do this at least once a month."

"I'm in," Sage said.

"So am I," Paige responded.

Later, while getting pedicures, Sage smiled at Paige and said, "Looks like you and Keith are getting along really well. I hear that you are all he talks about."

"He is such a sweetheart. I really like him. Like, a lot."

Meredith and Sage chuckled.

Three hours later, the three of them sat down on the sofa in Sage's den.

"I feel like a new woman," Paige stated.

"So do I," Meredith said in agreement. "I love pampering myself."

Paige checked her watch. "I need to go get my baby. I really enjoyed spending the day with you two. Let's do it again real soon. You ladies are, like, the only two friends I have in this entire state."

Sage walked her to the door.

When she returned, Meredith was on the telephone with Dale.

"That man is driving me crazy," Meredith announced

when she hung up. "I know he loves me, but I'm beginning to think that he doesn't want to marry me."

"Why do you feel that way?" Sage inquired.

"He keeps trying to push it out further. Now he thinks we should wait until he's been with a firm for at least a year."

"Does he know that you're ready to get married now?"

Meredith nodded. "I don't know what to do. I love him so much, but I'm tired of waiting for a wedding ring."

"I don't think you should give him an ultimatum unless you are prepared for it to go either way," Sage stated.

She hugged Meredith. "Just know that you and Dale have to find a way to get on the same page. I hope that it works out for you."

"So do I," Meredith whispered.

"He would be a fool to let you go. You are a sweetheart, and I want you to know that I love you, cousin. If Dale is the man that I think he is then he won't risk losing you."

Rising to her feet, Meredith said, "I hate to leave, but I have to meet my mother. She wants my help in selecting some wallpaper."

"Call me later if you need to talk," Sage told her.

"Thank you, Sage. I love you."

She walked Meredith to the door.

They were becoming closer every day. No one else in the DePaul family had come around, but Sage believed that it was only a matter of time.

Chapter 15

Sage heard the familiar sound of her mother's bracelets jingling as she walked toward her. "Sweetie, is everything all right? You look as if you have something weighing heavy on your mind."

She gave a slight nod. "Mama, everything's fine."

Barbara eyed her. "You sure?"

Sage pasted a smile on her face. "Actually, things are great in my world. My life couldn't be any better."

"Does this have anything to do with Ryan?"

"Yes, it does," she confirmed. "He is such a wonderful man, Mama. I just wish that my brothers were as happy for me as I am. I know that they are being protective, but hasn't Ryan proven himself already? Blaze and I used to do stuff together, but whenever I mention bringing Ryan around, he backs out on me."

"Maybe it's because Blaze doesn't want to feel like a third wheel," Barbara suggested.

"I guess I hadn't really looked at it that way," Sage admitted. "It's just that I love Ryan. I want him welcomed into the family in the same way that we welcomed Natasha."

Her mother nodded in understanding. "I must admit that he has done an exceptional job," Barbara stated, "which is why I can't help but wonder why he wasn't able to secure employment."

"There are a lot of people who possess great skills and wonderful résumés but are unable to get jobs," Sage pointed out. "The economy is really crazy right now.

"You are still not sure about him," Sage stated. "You don't really trust him, do you?"

Barbara met her gaze. "Ryan has proven to be a valuable member of our staff, but I do want you to be careful, Sage. Although he appears to be a hard worker, we do not know anything about this man."

"That's just it, Mama. I do know Ryan. My heart knew his the moment our paths crossed. I felt our connection instantly, and so did he. I trust Ryan. I just wish you all felt the same way."

"Give us time," Barbara said. "If Ryan is all that you say he is then we will see it for ourselves."

Sage was not her usual self, Ryan noted. "Long day?"

She glanced up at him. "Huh?"

"You look like you have something weighing on your mind."

"I had a conversation with my mother today," Sage said. "About you."

"What happened?" he asked.

"They are still wary of you, Ryan. I keep telling them

that they don't have to be," she told him. "I just wish they would trust me. You and I have no secrets. I don't understand why they are acting this way."

"Maybe it's because they only see me as an employee, Sage. I really haven't spent much time around them outside the hotel."

"I didn't bring you around them because I didn't want them making you uncomfortable," Sage explained.

"I am not afraid to face your family," he told her. "Sweetheart, I do not want to come between you and your family. I love you but I won't put you in a position where you would have to choose."

"You would break up with me if it came to that?"

Ryan nodded. "Family is important, Sage. I would never want you to give up your family for me. I'm not worth it."

"You are an incredible man," she murmured. "I owe you an apology, Ryan."

"For what?"

"I thought I was protecting you from my family. I should have brought you around them so that they could get to know you better. I'm so sorry."

"No apology is needed."

"We're going to Pacific Palisades this weekend," Sage announced. "It's time my family had a chance to see another side of you."

Ryan smiled. "Are you sure about this?"

"Yes. I love you, and I want them to understand why I love you so much."

After making love, Sage watched Ryan as he lay sleeping.

He was in her blood.

She eased out of bed and went downstairs to call Meredith. She had called Sage earlier. This was the first chance that Sage had to return the call.

"Hey, what's up?"

"Dale and I had a long talk. I was honest with him. I told him that I didn't want to wait much longer to get married."

"How did it go?"

"First he said that he needed to get some air to clear his head. He was gone for almost an hour. Sage, I wasn't sure if he was coming back."

"But he did come back, right?" Sage inquired.

"He did," Meredith responded.

"When he came back, he told me that he loved me and didn't want to risk losing me. Sage, he pulled out this tiny box and then asked me to marry him."

"Really? That's wonderful, Meredith."

"Can you believe it? I'm engaged, and we're going to get married next June."

Sage's eyes filled with tears. "I'm so happy for you, Meredith." She wiped her eyes. "This is truly good news. We're going to have to celebrate."

Meredith laughed. "I know. I've wanted this for so long that it hasn't fully sunk in yet. I'm still waiting to wake up from this beautiful dream."

"It's not a dream, sweetie. You are getting married, girl."

They talked for a few minutes more before ending the call.

Sage went back into the bedroom.

Ryan was still sleeping.

She gazed lovingly at him for a moment before removing her robe.

Sage eased into bed with Ryan, who stirred slightly, and then snuggled up against him.

Smiling, she closed her eyes.

She was thrilled for Meredith. She and Ryan were closer than ever; this was one of the happiest moments in her life. It could only get better from here, she decided.

Ryan and Sage drove out to Pacific Palisades.

He was not nervous about the visit but decided to proceed with caution. He did not want to inadvertently validate their suspicion.

Apparently, they were the last to arrive, because Ari and Natasha were in the house. Blaze was out on the patio with Malcolm, and Drayden was in the kitchen with his mother and a young woman who Ryan assumed was his girlfriend.

He and Sage greeted everyone and then headed outside.

Blaze pointed to a basketball. "Ryan, if you are going to start coming around, we need to see if you can play b-ball. I hope you bought balling clothes with you. Since Kellen's not here, we need a fourth, but you have to be worthy."

Ryan chuckled. "I'm always ready to play basketball. I keep playing clothes with me—at least I used to before things changed." He chose his words carefully.

Blaze eyed him. "You and I look about the same size. You can change into some of mine."

"I don't know about the rest of y'all, but I'm watching this game," Sage said when Natasha and Barbara joined them on the patio.

"So am I," Drayden's girlfriend contributed.

"Looks like we have a game," Malcolm said. "Everybody to the court. As usual, I'm the referee, and I'll accept no heckling from the fans." He glanced over at his wife.

Sage laughed.

They all walked over to the basketball court. The women sat in the stands while the men got ready.

"Can Ryan play basketball?" Natasha asked in a low voice.

Sage shrugged. "I have no idea. I've never seen him play." She realized that there was still more she had to learn about Ryan. She had no idea what sports he played, if any.

The men walked out on the court. Ryan had changed into a pair of red Nike shorts with a matching shirt. He had a pair of brand-new Nike shoes on his feet.

Sage glanced over at Blaze, who smiled and winked at her. Her brothers were making an effort with Ryan, which pleased her greatly.

They all whistled when Malcolm strolled out to the court dressed in a striped shirt and black shorts. Back home in Georgia, he used to referee youth basketball games.

Seconds into the game, Ryan scored three points.

"Yes," Sage screamed. "That's how you do it, baby."

Natasha grinned. "I had a feeling that he could ball."

Ryan scored another three points.

"So what do you boys think now?" Sage yelled. "Looks like my man is dominating on the court."

"He's made all of six points," Ari yelled back. "I wouldn't say he's dominating anything."

Ryan then scored two more points.

"I can't hear you," Sage teased. "Ryan, show them how it's done, baby. Take it to the hoop."

Blazed scored off a rebound.

"He's got skills," Ari responded after trying to catch his breath. "I'll give him that. The man can play some ball."

The game was almost over with the two teams tied.

Natasha screamed when Ari scored the winning shot. "That's it, baby."

"Lucky break," Sage said with a chuckle.

Sweaty, the men walked off the court.

Sage wrinkled up her nose when Ryan made his way to her. "Good game, sweetie, but talk to me after you shower."

Natasha did the same. She sent Ari straight to the showers.

As soon as the men showered and changed clothes, they gathered in the family room.

When Ryan entered the room, Ari walked over to him and said, "We can see how much you make our sister happy. It's clear that she loves you, Ryan. It's also very clear how much you love her, so there's really only one thing we can say and that's 'welcome to the family.'"

Sage wiped a tear from her eye. She was touched by her brother's gesture and told him so.

"We just want to make sure that you are loved as much as we love you, sis."

Later that evening, they headed back to Beverly Hills.

"I am so blown away by what happened today," Ryan

said in the car as they drove along the freeway. "I really enjoyed hanging out with your brothers and your parents." He chuckled. "Your dad takes his refereeing seriously, doesn't he?"

Sage nodded. "I'm so glad that we did this. I love my family, and I want them to love you as much as I do. They made the effort to get to know you outside of work. I'm so proud of them."

"Today really meant a lot to you."

"It did. We are a close family. I was beginning to feel as if we were growing apart, and I didn't like it."

Ryan reached over and took her by the hand. "I don't think you'll ever have to worry about something like that. Your family adores you, Sage. I can see how much they mean to you. That's why I would never come between you and them."

"I'm so glad that I don't have to worry about choosing."

As far as Sage was concerned, today had been perfect. She meant what she had told Ryan. She was very proud of the efforts made by her brothers. They were willing to put aside their own misgivings about Ryan for her happiness.

They would soon come to realize that she had been right all along about Ryan.

Chapter 16

Sage opened her door to find Ryan standing there looking quite handsome in a black suit she helped him pick out when they were out shopping earlier.

He openly admired the strapless black dress he had chosen for her. It hugged her curves in all of the right places, as if it had been custom-made for her body. "Sage, you look beautiful."

"So do you," she responded with a smile.

He had rented a car for the evening. When the valet brought it to them, Ryan escorted her to the car and then opened the door to the passenger side. He walked around to the driver side and got in.

He drove them to Marina Del Rey where they had reservations at an oceanfront restaurant.

They ordered drinks while they waited for their food to arrive.

Sage ordered an apple martini while he decided on a glass of iced tea. "This place is beautiful."

Ryan agreed. "But it doesn't come close to your beauty."

"How did I get so lucky?" Sage wondered aloud.

"I'm the lucky one, Sage," Ryan interjected. "My life was crazy until you came along. You literally changed my circumstances and my life in general. Until I met you, I never thought I could love a person as deeply as I love you."

"I keep waiting for the other shoe to fall," she confessed. "Things are just so perfect between us. Do you think it is going to be like this forever?"

"I will do everything I can to make sure that you are always this happy."

Their food arrived.

Sage had ordered the grilled salmon while Ryan chose the steak and lobster entrée.

She sampled her salmon. "This is delicious."

He sliced off a piece of his steak and stuck it in his mouth.

"How is it?" she asked. "It looks good. I'll have to try that the next time."

Ryan sliced off a piece and placed it on Sage's plate. "You can try it now," he told her.

"I've been thinking that since you are at my place most of the time—why don't you move in?" Sage wiped her mouth on the edge of her napkin. "It's just a thought."

"I appreciate the offer," he told her. "Sage, I love you, and as much as I enjoy waking up with you, I think it's too soon for me to move in. The truth is that I would rather wait until we had a more permanent union."

"Permanent…like marriage?"

Ryan met her gaze. "You seem surprised. Sage, I am not dating you just because. I would like to have a future with you. At least, I'm assuming that we are both thinking along those lines."

"Definitely," she responded. "I do want to get married."

"Just a few short months ago, the last thing on my mind was getting married. It was not in any of my future plans, but you changed that, as well."

After dinner, they returned to the penthouse.

When they entered the master bedroom, Sage turned around to face Ryan. She kissed him, her curves molding to the contours of his body. He savored the warmth of her kiss, leaving him burning with fire and sending his body in a wild swirl.

She kissed him hungrily.

"Sage…I love you so much."

The anguish she heard in his voice caught Sage unaware. The love they shared was passionate and intense. They were a part of each other.

For a brief moment, she silently considered, *How can I ever give my heart to another man if my relationship with Ryan does not work out?*

She did not want to ruin the moment, so she forced the thought to the back of her mind. Right now, all Sage wanted to do was give herself to Ryan, mind, body and soul.

Sage and Ryan strolled into the private dining room of Le Magnifique for a family dinner. Several guests had come into town a few days early for Ari and Natasha's wedding on Saturday. Her younger siblings, Zaire and Kellen, had arrived earlier in the day, and Sage could not wait to see them. She hated that they were three thousand miles away. She was used to seeing them at her parents' home on the weekends when they were in Georgia.

She broke into a grin when she spied her sister across the room with their father. Taking Ryan by the hand, she said, "I want to introduce you to my sister." Sage led him over to where her father and Zaire stood.

"Zaire, I'd like you to meet Ryan," she said, making the introductions.

Her sister smiled. "It's so nice to finally meet you." Zaire glanced at Sage and then added, "He's cuter than you said."

"Zaire, he can hear you," Sage uttered. She gave Ryan a tiny smile in embarrassment.

They were soon joined by Kellen, who introduced himself to Ryan without preamble.

The two men shook hands.

Kellen embraced Sage. "You look beautiful, sis."

"Thanks. You look quite handsome yourself."

"You sound surprised," he responded with a grin. "You know how I do."

Sage shook her head. "Kellen, you will never change."

"Why should I?" he responded. "I'm perfection."

Zaire groaned while Sage pretended to gag.

"I love the closeness that you share with your family," Ryan told her as they settled down in the family room.

Sage raised her eyes to his. "Ryan, are you close to your family? You never really talk about them."

He shook his head no. "The only time we really

get together is when there is a death in the family. We always talk about getting together, but it never happens."

"I guess someone in your family needs to make the first move," Sage suggested. "You know…to get together."

Ryan seemed to consider her words. "You may be right. We've all been waiting on that person to initiate the gathering. In the end, no one has done anything about it."

"You could be that person," Sage suggested.

He gave a slight nod. "You're right."

Standing beside Ryan, Sage openly admired him. He stood tall and regal, looking very handsome in a black tux that embraced his body as if it had been designed just for him. It was hard to believe that he was the same man who was homeless just a few short months ago.

There was no doubt in Sage's mind that Ryan was the best-looking man in the restaurant. She wove her fingers through his, a warm contrast against the coolness of his copper-colored skin. Sage realized with certain clarity that she loved Ryan more than life itself and never tired of looking at him.

Zaire strolled toward them. "Ryan, do you mind if I borrow my sister for a moment?"

He smiled. "Not at all."

"I'll be right back," Sage promised.

"He's very handsome," Zaire told her sister. "And you are glowing up something. I thought Natasha was supposed to be the one walking on clouds. Well, she isn't alone."

Sage chuckled. "What are you talking about?"

"You're in love with Ryan," Zaire announced. "Girl, it's written all over that face of yours."

"Really?"

Zaire nodded. "I'm happy for you, sis."

"Thank you," Sage murmured.

They embraced.

Sage glanced over her shoulder to where Ryan and her father stood. They appeared to be engaged in deep conversation.

Turning around to face Zaire, she asked, "Do you think I need to rescue Ryan?"

Her sister shook her head no. "He looks like he can handle himself just fine. Besides, Daddy likes him a lot. Everyone has nothing but good things to say about Ryan. Sage, you have nothing to worry about."

Sage broke into a grin. "Zaire, you're absolutely right. I don't have a thing to worry about where Ryan is concerned."

She spotted Meredith at the door and walked over to greet her. "I'm so glad you came."

"Dale came with me. He wanted to meet everyone."

Sage's mouth dropped open in surprise. "Really?"

Meredith nodded. "He went to the men's room, but he'll be right back."

Dale joined them, and Meredith introduced him to Sage.

"I'll introduce you to the family," she told them.

Ryan stood back and watched Sage as she went around the room with Meredith DePaul and her fiancé. He was impressed with the way that she had set aside her own feelings and given Meredith a chance to prove herself.

She was the angel of second chances, he decided.

My sweet angel.

"What are you doing over here by yourself?" Zaire asked. "Are you having a nice time?"

He nodded. "I am. I have to confess that I am a people watcher. I tend to stay in the background."

"I'm glad. I was hoping my family hadn't run you away with a million questions."

Ryan laughed. "They haven't. Actually, they really haven't asked me anything outside of my intentions toward Sage."

"We're very protective of one another."

"I can see that."

"However, we do not interfere in each other's relationships—at least we try not to do it."

"It's clear that you all have accepted Natasha into your family."

Zaire nodded. "Ari loves her, and she loves him. I want him to be happy. I want the same thing for Sage."

Ryan nodded in understanding.

"I'm going to see if I can rescue your girlfriend. It will give me a chance to get to know Meredith. Sage is way more forgiving than I am, but she is usually right about people, so I'm going to trust her instincts."

"Meredith is good people," Ryan told her. "She really wants to get to know this side of her family. She's not like the rest of the DePauls."

"I'm willing to give her a chance," Zaire said. "But I won't withdraw caution until I'm a hundred percent sure that she isn't trying to play us."

"Zaire, I've told you that Meredith is nothing like her brother," Sage said as she joined them.

"I said I'll give her a chance, and I mean it."

Sage glanced over her shoulder to where Meredith was sitting with Dale. "You're going to like her."

Zaire did not look convinced.

Sage glanced up at Ryan, who shrugged. "You have to give them time," he told her.

The next day, Sage's schedule was a busy one.

She had meetings back-to-back, one of which started late, so she had to cancel her lunch with Ryan. However, she promised to meet him for dinner at her place.

Sage left the office shortly after five. She wanted to get dinner started so that it would be ready by the time Ryan arrived. She chose a simple meal of baked chicken, broccoli, rice and yeast rolls.

Ryan showed up promptly at six o'clock.

He greeted her with a kiss. "You were really busy today. We could have eaten at the restaurant so you wouldn't have to worry about cooking."

"I didn't mind. I know how much you enjoy a home-cooked meal," Sage responded.

After dinner, they settled down and watched a movie together.

She laid her head against Ryan's chest. Sage really enjoyed moments like this—she and Ryan cuddled up together watching television or a movie. She could not have asked for a better evening.

It took her a moment to realize that Ryan had fallen asleep.

Sage eased away from him and rose to her feet. She went into the bedroom and removed her clothes.

She showered quickly and then slipped on a silky nightgown.

Sage slowly turned the doorknob and opened her door, peeking to see if Ryan had awakened. He was still sleeping. "Poor baby," she whispered.

At the far end of the room, a floor-to-ceiling window gifted her with a looking glass to the beauty of Beverly Hills at night. Sage crossed the varnished hardwood floor in bare feet toward the rich ebony bed that framed an amethyst-colored comforter and several pillows in gray.

Sage sat down on the bed and leaned back against the stack of pillows adorning the king-size headboard.

There was a soft knock on her door.

"Ryan," she called out.

He stuck his head inside. "It's me. I'm sorry about falling asleep. I didn't realize that I was so tired."

She awarded him a tiny smile. "Honey, it's fine. Come to bed."

Walking inside the room, Ryan's eyes traveled from her face, to her neck and then continued downward. "You look stunning," he whispered.

A few minutes later, Ryan was bare-chested, and the light from the moon cast a soft glow over his firm muscles. He joined her in bed, tracing his fingertip across her lip, which caused her skin to tingle when he touched her. He paused to kiss her, sending currents of desire through Sage.

"Make love to me," she whispered between kisses.

Ryan groaned softly. He bent his head and captured her lips in a demanding kiss. Locking her hands behind his neck, Sage returned his kiss, matching passion for passion.

"You are so beautiful," he told her in a husky voice.

As the clock stoke midnight, Ryan and Sage rode a golden wave of pleasure.

Chapter 17

I can't do this any longer. I cannot continue to keep secrets from Sage.

She deserved the truth and not only that—she deserved better from him. Ryan decided he was going to throw caution to the wind and tell Sage everything, including the real reason behind his stay in California.

He had no idea how she would respond, but he had to go through with his decision. One thing was for sure: he had to be honest with Sage before they could take their relationship to the next level. Ryan was ready to propose. He wanted to make her his wife.

I'm going to tell her the truth after the wedding. If she's still speaking to me, I'll ask her to marry me.

"Hey, you…"

Ryan glanced up from his computer monitor. "What are you doing here?"

Sage sat down in one of the visitor chairs. "I got tired

of waiting for you to come to me, so I figured if we had any chance of leaving here before nightfall that I had to come get you. We have a wedding rehearsal and dinner to attend. Did you forget?"

He checked his watch. "Sage, I'm sorry. I let time get away from me."

Ryan rushed to his feet. "I'm ready."

She surveyed his face. "Everything okay?"

Ryan pasted on a smile. "I'm fine, sweetheart. Let's get out of here." He ignored the wave of apprehension he felt. He was not looking forward to this talk with Sage, but it was something he could no longer put off. But for now, he intended to make sure that she enjoyed the pre-wedding parties and the ceremony. Afterward, he was going to confess all. Sage was going to be disappointed in him, but Ryan hoped that it would not last too long. She had a very forgiving spirit, and he prayed that she would be able to understand his reasons for the deception and forgive him.

Barbara had the grounds of the home decorated to set the tone for Ari and Natasha's wedding. She had rose petal initials of the couple's first names plotted on the lawn, mirroring the monogrammed invitations.

Guests were greeted with sheaves of wheat at the entrance of the huge tent. Flowers and fabrics in the traditional fall color scheme of reds, oranges, browns and yellows were used as decorations throughout. Handmade fans featuring the monograms on top of a diamond grid motif, created by a local artist to represent the paned windows of the Alexander mansion, were given to each guest to double as the perfect keepsake and ceremony program.

Large displays of mums, roses, daisies, yarrow, tallow berries and natural wheat were placed at the front of the house and around the back where a huge white tent had been placed for the ceremony.

All of the ushers and groomsmen looked elegant in their tuxedos adorned with boutonnieres made of a mum accented with a pheasant feather and a spray of wheat.

Barbara met with the florist and the wedding coordinator to make sure that everything was as it should be.

Sage glanced at the clock and rushed out to get her mother. It was time for her to get ready for the wedding. The hairstylist had arrived and was waiting for Barbara in the master bedroom.

"Mama, you need to get ready," Sage told her. "Everything looks wonderful."

"This is Ari's wedding," Barbara stated. "It has to be perfect."

Sage slipped an arm around her mother and said, "Mama, it is perfect. However, if you are not ready when it's time for the ceremony to start…"

Barbara nodded. "Okay, sweetie. Let's get inside. I don't want to be late for my son's wedding."

Sage released a soft sigh of relief. Her mother was a perfectionist, but when it came to weddings, she was obsessed even more. When Ari married April, they had a small traditional church ceremony, but it didn't matter to Barbara. She still insisted on making sure that it was perfect and romantic.

After making sure her mother was in the master suite getting dressed, Sage joined the other bridesmaids.

"Where have you been?" Zaire questioned. "Natasha has been looking for you."

"I had to make sure that Mama would be ready in time for the ceremony," she responded. "You know what a perfectionist she can be when it comes to weddings or parties."

Zaire nodded in agreement. "C'mon, we need to change."

Sage followed her sister into a nearby bedroom.

"You were right about Meredith," Zaire commented as she removed her robe. "We had lunch together yesterday. I like her. She told me about her upcoming wedding to Dale. What's he really like?"

Sage slipped out of her sundress. "He's great, and it's clear that he loves Meredith," she murmured with a smile. "He makes her very happy."

"Ryan's doing a great job of making you happy."

Sage walked over to the closet and removed the hanger, holding her dress off the door. She glanced over her shoulder in Zaire's direction. "I think he's the one—the one man for me."

"I'm not surprised," her sister said with a grin.

A few minutes later, both Zaire and Sage were dressed. Zaire stood in front of the bathroom mirror and fingered her spiral curls, while she studied her reflection in the mirror hanging on the wall above the tall oak chest of drawers.

Sage surveyed her sister. "You look beautiful, Zaire."

"So do you, sis. Natasha chose the perfect bridesmaid dress. I have to give it to her."

Natasha's sister, Natalie, knocked softly before opening the door. "You ladies ready?"

"Yes," they said in unison.

"How is Natasha?" Sage asked.

"She's all nervous and worried that something is going to go wrong." Natalie handed Sage and Zaire bouquets that consisted of five roses that had been stripped of leaves and thorns and were surrounded by white tulips, snapdragons and lilies of the valley. The stems were wrapped with a beautiful bow.

Sage made her way to the door. "I'm going to go have a little talk with Natasha. Nothing is going to ruin this day for her. I won't let it."

What is she doing here?

Ryan's mouth dropped open in surprise when he glimpsed his ex-wife and her new husband making their way down the aisle. Ryan hadn't expected to see her at Ari's wedding. He had no idea that Sandra even knew the Alexander family.

She was probably here only because of her husband. Ryan could understand why he had received an invitation.

Ryan turned around to avoid meeting Sandra's gaze. It amazed him that he had actually had feelings for her once upon a time. How could he have ever loved such a selfish, manipulative woman?

Someone walked up behind him.

Ryan turned around expecting to come face to face with Sandra. He was pleasantly surprised to find Sage standing there.

"Why are you out here? I thought you'd be with the bride."

"I just came out here to check on you."

"I'm fine, baby."

She smiled. "I have to go, but I'll see you right after the wedding ceremony."

He met her gaze. "I'll be here."

"I love you, Ryan."

He smiled at her. "I love you, too."

It was killing Ryan inside at the thought of disappointing Sage. She loved him unconditionally.

Harold walked into the tent as if he owned it. The last time he had been at the estate home was the day that his uncle died. Now it belonged to Malcolm Alexander. He glanced around, recognizing many of the high-profile guests who had come to witness Ari and Natasha's wedding.

Meredith had received an invitation to the wedding but he had not. However, he was not going to let that discourage him from attending. If anyone asked, Harold was prepared to tell him or her that he was here as Meredith's guest. It didn't matter that she was here with her fiancé.

Harold wanted to attend because he genuinely cared for Natasha and wanted her to be happy, although he did not entirely approve of her choice in a husband.

The ceremony was about to begin.

Harold sat down across from Ryan. He wasn't surprised at all to see him among the guests. He knew all about Sage's boyfriend. She had literally taken to the streets to find him.

Meredith sat down beside him. "What are you doing here?"

"I came to support Natasha on her wedding day," he replied smoothly.

"You were not invited, Harold," his sister pointed out.

"Sure I was," he countered. "*You* invited me as your guest.

"Your fiancé looks lonely. I think you should join him."

"Harold, please don't do anything to ruin this day for them."

He acted as if he did not hear her.

Meredith got up and walked over to where Dale was sitting. Harold stole a peek at her. She glared at him for a moment and then turned away.

Harold's mouth tightened.

He and his baby sister used to be close, but their relationship changed once she hooked up with Sage Alexander. They had already taken so much from him.

Harold vowed to find a way to change that.

Natasha floated down the aisle on her father's arm toward the man she would love forever.

Moments later, she and Ari stood facing each other as they said their vows.

Natasha spoke first. "Ari, I take you to be my husband. I will trust you and respect you, laugh with you and cry with you, loving you faithfully through good times and bad, regardless of the obstacles we may face together. I give you my hand, my heart and my love from this day forward for as long as we both shall live."

"Natasha, I give myself to you in marriage. I want you to know that I eagerly anticipate the chance to grow together, getting to know the woman you will become and falling in love a little more every day. I promise to encourage and inspire you, to laugh with you and to comfort you in times of sorrow and struggle. I promise to love and cherish you through whatever life may bring us all the days of our lives."

Sage fought back tears as she listened to Ari and Natasha pledge their lives to one another.

"I now pronounce you man and wife...."

Ari pulled Natasha into his arms, drawing her close. He pressed his lips to hers for a chaste yet meaningful kiss. A few minutes later, he escorted his new wife down the aisle and through the double exit doors at the back of the church. They escaped into a nearby room, waiting until it was time to go back into the chapel for the wedding photographs.

The wedding party joined them a few minutes later.

Natasha broke into a big smile when Sage walked over to them. "We're married." She held up her left hand to show off the wedding set. "I can truly say that this is the happiest day of my life."

Sage embraced her new sister-in-law. "Congratulations."

When they came out for pictures, Sage looked around for Ryan. She found him talking to Meredith and Dale.

He greeted her with a kiss.

"It was a beautiful ceremony," she murmured.

Meredith agreed.

Sage heard someone call her name, and said, "Back to bridesmaid duty."

She spotted Harold DePaul and headed in his direction. "Who let you in here?"

He boldly met her gaze. "I'm a guest…the same as everyone else."

"I don't believe that for a minute," Sage responded. "I have to go, but if you do anything to try and mess this up for Natasha and Ari, I'll deal with you myself."

"I suppose I should be afraid," he responded.

Sage met his gaze straight on. "*Very* afraid." She was not going to upset Ari or Natasha, but she intended to let her father know that Harold was there.

Chapter 18

Ryan felt a tap on his shoulder. He turned around to face Sandra.

"I thought it was you, but I couldn't be sure," she said. "What on earth are you doing here?"

"I could ask you the same question," he retorted. "Do you even know the Alexander family?"

She shrugged in nonchalance. "No, but I'm sure I'll be running into them." She held up her left hand, showing off her huge diamond engagement ring and sparkling wedding band. "We do run in the same circles."

Ryan stared at her in disgust.

"I'm really surprised to see you here, though," she said. "How did you snag an invitation to this wedding?"

"I know someone," he responded.

"Ryan, I know that you're still very angry with me, but I hope that one day we can get past all this."

"I am no longer angry, Sandra. I just hope you were

more truthful with your husband this time around. If not, I assure you that this marriage won't last either. Do yourself a favor and just be honest."

Sandra bristled at his words. "How dare you," she uttered.

Ryan shrugged. "It was just a word of advice. It's up to you whether or not you accept it," he stated.

"I know that you don't believe me, but I did love you, Ryan." Sandra dabbed at her eyes with a napkin.

Ryan was not buying her act. "You may have loved me, but you loved yourself more. It was all about you, Sandra. There was no room in your life for me or for children."

"You need to accept the fact that I wasn't ready for a child, Ryan."

"It doesn't matter anymore, Sandra. In fact, it turned out for the best. The last thing either one of us needed was to be tied for life because of a child."

Sandra did not respond.

"Am I interrupting?" Sage inquired.

Ryan shook his head. "I've been waiting for you, sweetheart."

Sandra's mouth dropped open in shock.

"It was nice talking to you. Enjoy the rest of your evening," he told her before leaving with Sage.

"Who was that woman?" Sage asked him when they sat down at their table.

"She is married to some movie producer," Ryan responded. "Her name is Sandra."

Sage glanced over her shoulder. "Oh, that's Frank Miller's new wife."

Ryan was ready to leave the reception. He did not

like having his past so close, especially when she could blow everything for him. Ryan prayed she would keep her mouth closed. He just needed to get through the rest of the evening and then Sage would know the truth.

Harold had watched the exchange between Frank Miller's bride and Ryan with interest. How in the world did a homeless man from New York get to know a woman like that? He saw that there was an empty seat at Miller's table.

He made his way over to the table where Frank sat with his wife, Sandra. Harold did not know her but had seen her at several events and premieres.

"I wonder what he's doing here in California," Sandra was saying to her husband. "He has always hated it here."

"I really don't care as long as it has nothing to do with us," Frank responded.

Harold followed her gaze. She was definitely referring to Ryan.

This is getting interesting.

When Frank got up to get her a glass of champagne, Harold asked, "Do you know Ryan Manning?"

She nodded. "Oh, I know him quite well. I was married to him."

"Really?" Harold found it interesting that she would admit to having been married to a man who was living on the streets up until a few months ago. "You were married to Ryan?"

"Yes," Sandra responded. "Our marriage didn't work because he was always on the road chasing one story or another."

Harold gave her a perplexed look. "I'm sorry, but I'm confused here. The guy over there works at the Alexander-DePaul Hotel in Beverly Hills. He manages the new restaurant."

Sandra laughed. "Well, I'm not surprised. Ryan has always loved cooking, and he even owns a restaurant in New York, but his passion is his investigative reports. He wants to save the world through his writing."

"Ryan Manning is a writer?" Harold asked.

"Not only is he a writer but a well-known one," Frank chimed in as he handed the flute to his wife. "He writes under the pseudonym R. G. McCall."

"That's probably how he met the Alexanders," Sandra stated. "He is probably doing a story on them."

"Hmm," Harold murmured. He could not believe his good fortune. Harold was pretty sure that the Alexander family had no idea who was working right under their nose.

"Harold, what are you doing here?" Malcolm demanded, interrupting Harold's conversation with the Millers.

"Oh, I just assumed my invitation got lost somehow. After all, I am family and a close friend of Natasha. Why wouldn't I have been invited to the wedding?"

Malcolm glared at him but did not utter a response.

"I'm just sitting here enjoying the festivities and stimulating conversation with your guests."

"Make sure that's all you do," Malcolm stated. "We don't want any trouble out of you. I don't want to ruin the evening by kicking you out."

Harold gave him a smile that did not reach his eyes. "You don't have to worry about me. I am on my best behavior." He could feel the heat of his sister's gaze on him.

Malcolm navigated to the next table and spent a few minutes talking to the guests.

Harold struggled to contain his anger.

How dare Malcolm approach him like this and in front of the other guests? He had no right to humiliate him in this manner. He was going to find a way to bring Malcolm down a peg or two. First, he was going to deal with Sage and Ryan.

Harold rose to his feet and quickly navigated over to where Ryan was standing in line at the bar.

Ryan greeted him and then proceeded to order a glass of wine.

"I have to admit that you had me fooled completely," Harold stated, a fake smile on his face. "I had no idea that it was you."

Ryan was instantly on his guard. "I'm afraid I don't have any idea what you're talking about. Look, I don't know you, but I've heard a lot about you, Harold. None of it was very nice."

He grinned. "Oh, I think you know exactly what I'm talking about, Ryan. Your ex-wife had an awful lot to say about you."

He muttered a curse. That woman had no right to open her mouth.

Harold leaned forward and whispered in his ear. "Tell me something, Ryan…what really brings you to Los Angeles?"

Ryan turned around to face Harold DePaul. "My reasons for being in Los Angeles have nothing to do with you. Now stay away from me."

"Why so rude? I thought we could become friends."

"I don't need friends like you," Ryan retorted.

"You may one day decide differently."

Ryan sent him a sharp look. "I doubt it."

"Harold, I hope that you're not trying to start anything," Sage said from behind them.

"My dear sweet cousin, I think there is something you should know."

Ryan grabbed Harold by the arm. "This is not the time or the place."

"Let go of me."

"I don't want to make a scene or ruin this day for Ari and Natasha," Ryan stated. "If you want to finish this conversation, we can do it away from here."

Sage glanced from one man to the other. "What is going on between you two?" she asked in a loud whisper. "Harold, I'm pretty sure you weren't even invited to the wedding after what you did to Natasha. Why don't you just leave and stop trying to start drama?"

Harold sent her a hard look. "You're worried about me? That's actually funny. The man you should be concerned about is your boyfriend. By the way, has he introduced you to his ex-wife and her new husband?"

Sage gasped in shock. "Ryan, what is he talking about?"

He did not respond. Instead, Ryan glared at Harold, who seemed intent on causing trouble. His hands curled into fists.

"Ryan…" Sage pressed. "You were married before?"

"We can talk about this later tonight," he told her.

Sage shook her head no. "Why am I just hearing

about this now? What other secrets have you been keeping from me?"

Before Ryan could reply, Harold uttered, "It's funny you should ask that question."

"Shut up," Ryan snapped in anger.

He took Sage by the hand and asked, "Is there someplace we can talk?"

Harold was not about to be put off. He stood in their path, blocking their exit. "I have always enjoyed reading your articles, especially the one you did on the plight of military families."

Confused, Sage glanced up at the man standing beside her—the man she loved and thought she knew. "Ryan..."

He turned to face her. "There's something I had planned to tell you later, but I think we're past that now. I would rather not have this discussion out here."

"We can go inside the house and talk," Sage stated.

They made their way across the manicured grounds and into the house.

As soon as they were in the family room, Sage turned to Ryan and demanded, "Okay, so what is it that you have to tell me? Let's start with your ex-wife and the fact that you were married before."

Ryan could see the look of hurt on her face, and it bothered him. He loved Sage, and he hoped that they would be able to get past all he was about to confess.

"I should have told you about Sandra, but honestly, I had buried her and that marriage in my past and just didn't think about it anymore—especially after meeting you."

Sage sat down on the sofa. "I suppose I should have asked you if you were ever married."

"None of this is on you," Ryan said. "I take ownership in this situation. I was not completely honest with you about my life."

"Do you have children?" she queried.

"No," Ryan stated. "No children."

"Then what have you lied about?"

"I was never homeless," Ryan said, his eyes never leaving her face. She looked so hurt that it was unbearable. He was almost relieved when Sage finally looked away from him.

"I only pretended to be homeless for a project. I'm an investigative reporter."

She met his gaze. "So you were never a chef or had a restaurant. That was all a lie, as well."

Ryan shook his head. "That part is true. I have a very successful eatery in New York, and it's managed by my brother."

"You have a brother," she repeated.

"Sweetheart, I'm so sorry for hurting you."

"*Really*? You're really sorry for pretending to be someone you're not. You're sorry for playing me for a fool."

"It was never my intent to play you, Sage," he responded. "I hope that you know enough about me to recognize my true intentions."

"I don't think that I know you at all."

"Sweetheart, I love you."

"I feel that there is more to this story, so you might as well tell me everything, because if you don't I'm sure Harold will have no hesitation."

"Yes, please tell her," Harold urged with a grin as he entered the family room.

"What do you want?" Sage demanded.

"I came in to make sure that you're okay," he told her.

"My sister doesn't need you to check on her," Blaze said from behind them. "What's going on in here?" he asked.

"Ryan and I are having a *private* discussion," Sage stated. "Can you both just leave us alone to finish our conversation?"

Both Blaze and Harold remained rooted in the spots they were standing in. It was obvious they were not going to leave him and Sage alone.

"Sage, I am sorry to see you so upset, but I felt you needed to know the truth about this man," Harold told her before adding, "R.G....sorry about that. You're going by Ryan Manning these days."

Sage glared at Ryan. "What is your real name?"

"I am Ryan Manning. I never lied about that."

"Then why did Harold just call you R.G.?" She paused a moment as recognition set in. "You're R. G. McCall." Sage shook her head in despair. "Ryan, please tell me that I'm wrong," she whispered.

"Sweetheart, I'm sorry."

Blaze grabbed Harold, edging him toward the front door. "It's time for you to leave."

"Hey, don't hate the messenger."

Sage rose to her feet and walked over to Harold. She slapped him and then said, "That's my way of showing gratitude for what you did today. You are such a miserable man that you'd do anything to make sure everyone around you feels the same. If you thought you'd get to see me cry, then you are sadly mistaken."

"*Leave?* Why should I leave?" Harold asked in mock dismay. "It looks like the party is just getting started."

"You did what you set out to do, so get out of here," Ryan stated in a tone that brooked no argument. "Leave now before you get hurt!"

Blaze agreed.

After Harold left the house, Sage met Ryan's gaze with eyes that were bright with unshed tears. She shook her head sadly before walking out of the room.

He was about to go after her but was stopped by Blaze.

"Leave her alone, Ryan," he stated. "You've caused her enough pain for now. This is my brother's wedding day, and I don't intend to ruin it for the rest of the family. However, you and I will have a conversation very soon."

"I'm fine with that," Ryan responded. "I love Sage, and I'm not going to give up on what we have."

Sage sat on the edge of her bed and wiped away her tears.

She felt like such a fool for ever believing in Ryan. He was a complete fraud, and she had fallen for his deceit hook, line and sinker.

"I used to be a pretty good judge of character," she whispered. *Maybe he was right about some women being desperate. If I hadn't wanted to find a husband so badly, I would've realized sooner that he was lying to me.*

"Hey, are you okay?" Zaire asked from the doorway of the guest bedroom. "I saw you and Ryan come into the house. You two looked like you were about to have an intense conversation."

"Did he leave?" Sage asked.

"I think so," Zaire answered. "What was Harold doing here? I'm pretty sure he wasn't on the guest list."

"He wanted to make sure that I knew Ryan was making a fool out of me. I found out that he was just using me to get a story."

"I don't believe that for a second about Ryan," her sister responded quickly. "I've seen the way he looks at you, Sage. That man has real feelings for you. I'm kind of surprised at you. You are always so forgiving."

She didn't want to hear it. "Ryan would've told me the truth if he cared anything about me. He would have come clean about his identity. Oh, he's the mysterious R. G. McCall, and his ex-wife is here. She's here with her new husband. I never even knew that he was married before."

"I can't stand Harold DePaul," Zaire uttered. "He hates to see us with any amount of happiness."

"I can't blame Harold for this situation, Zaire. This is all Ryan's fault." Sage met her sister's concerned gaze. "I'll never forgive him for this."

Sage decided to spend the night with her parents.

Ryan had already called twice and announced that he would drop by her penthouse when he thought she would be home, but she wasn't ready to see or talk to him. Sage needed some time to process all that had happened.

She was hurt, confused and angry.

How could she be so foolish? Sage knew that something had been off with Ryan, but she had believed in him and his lies. She had actually believed that he had not been on the streets long, which explained why he was missing that forlorn look that so many of the homeless wore. Then there was the fact of his strong muscletoned body…

Sage tried to close her mind from thoughts of Ryan. The betrayal stung, the venom of anger spreading through her body like a wildfire.

There was a soft knock on the bedroom door.

Barbara peeked inside. "I just came up to check on you," she said.

"I'll be okay, Mama."

She smiled. "I know that, dear. But right now, you're experiencing a lot of emotions that you need to sort out."

Sage knew her mother was right. "I'm more hurt than angry. But the betrayal hurts worst of all."

"Have you given Ryan a chance to explain?"

"He's had one from the first moment I gave him a room to shower, clothing, food and a job. Ryan has had several opportunities to be honest with me. Mama, I don't think I can ever trust him again."

"I'm so sorry, dear," Barbara murmured. "I know how much you love this young man."

"I really wish I didn't,"

"But you do," her mother responded. "Because of that love, you have to talk to Ryan. Give him a chance to really explain his side of things. You need to do this for yourself. Trust me."

Sage's eyes filled with tears. "You don't intentionally deceive someone you love."

"No, you don't," her mother agreed. "But love can

conquer a multitude of sins, sweetie. We are all human and imperfect."

"It doesn't bother you that Ryan used me to get to our family? He's writing a story about us."

"We have nothing to hide."

"Mama, that's not the point."

Barbara sat down on the edge of the bed. "Honey, Ryan was wrong in the way he handled this situation, but I do believe with my entire heart that this man loves you dearly."

"I don't agree. If Ryan truly loved me, then he would've told the truth."

"Talk to Ryan," Barbara insisted. "You don't have to do it tonight, tomorrow or the day after that. Wait until you're ready."

"That day may never come," Sage commented. "Honesty and loyalty are very important to me. It's pretty obvious that Ryan failed in both areas."

Ryan was waiting in the hotel lobby when Sage arrived the next day.

"Sage, we need to talk," he said. "I want to get everything out in the open so that we can get past this."

She met his gaze and responded, "Ryan, there's really nothing to discuss. You lied to me. I cannot just brush it off and keep moving. I'm not wired that way."

He followed her to the elevator and up to her office.

"It wasn't like that, Sage," Ryan stated. "I just didn't tell you that I was a reporter for good reason. I always keep my identity a secret, but because of the way I feel about you, I had planned to tell you everything last night—only Harold DePaul beat me to it. You know his character, so you know why he did this."

"Ryan, you led me to believe that you were homeless. That was a lie. What does this say about your character?"

"I was on assignment," Ryan stated after a moment. "But, Sage, you've got to believe me. I never wanted to hurt you. When I began this ruse, I definitely didn't count on falling in love with you. Everything changed when my heart got involved."

"I feel like I can never trust you, Ryan."

He reached for her, but Sage stepped away from him. "Sweetheart, I want you to know that you can trust me."

"Please leave, Ryan," she whispered in a pained voice. "I just can't do this right now."

"I'm so sorry for hurting you, sweetheart. It was never my intent."

Sage didn't respond; she just kept her back turned to him. His betrayal still stung as much as the day before. Sage refused to let him see just how much his actions had wounded her. "Please, I want you to go."

"I'd like to stay on at the restaurant until you find another manager."

She wanted to refuse him, but the truth was that Ryan had been a great manager and they needed a strong presence in this new venture. "That's fine. I'll alert Personnel that we'll need to find your replacement immediately."

Ryan didn't seem to want to let the subject drop. "I never wanted you to find out this way."

"I'm not sure I would feel any differently regardless of when you told me," Sage admitted.

"I love you, Sage. I've never loved anyone as much as I love you. Please tell me that we can get through this with our relationship intact. I know that you need some space to deal with all this, but I don't want to lose you."

"Ryan, I can't talk about this right now. I'm not ready."

He backed away from her. "Okay, I'll give you space. But I want you to understand that I'm not just going to disappear. What we have together is special, and I'm not going to just give up on you."

Sage kept her expression blank until he left her office. She slowly turned the doorknob and opened her door, widening the exit. Cautiously, she walked into the hallway. At the far end was a floor-to-ceiling window that gifted Sage a picturesque view of Beverly Hills.

She navigated across the plush carpeting. Sage stood at the window looking out while fighting back tears. She loved Ryan with a fierceness that surprised even her.

Ryan says he loves me. Do I believe him?

The answer to that question was a difficult one for Sage. Ryan was willing to live on the streets in order to pursue material for his research. She truly believed he would do just about anything for a story, including leading her on.

The thought brought on more tears.

Sage made her way back to her office before anyone could see her crying. *What's wrong with me? Why am I crying over this man like this? He's so not worth it.*

She had just sat down at her desk when Blaze strolled in. "I wanted to check on you."

"I'm okay," Sage responded with a tiny smile.

"Where is Ryan?"

"He's probably at the restaurant."

"Why?"

"He asked if he could stay on until we found someone to replace him. I told him that it was fine."

Blaze shook his head. "He was hired under false pretenses. He should be fired."

"We have no one else to manage the restaurant, and it is a success partly because of Ryan."

"Sis, you have a kind heart, sweetheart. I'm ready to throw him out on his butt."

"My decision was based on business and not my personal relationship. Ryan did an excellent job, and I'm not going to take that away from him just because he kept secrets from me. Besides, we are already looking for a replacement for him."

"Good," Blaze uttered.

"I love you, Blaze, but this is between me and Ryan. I want you and everybody else to stay out of it."

"He was writing about all of us," her brother countered. "That gives us the right to be involved."

Sage released a long sigh.

Blaze checked his watch. "I have a meeting to get to, but call me if you feel like talking. If not, we can take in a movie or something. I don't think you should be alone right now."

"Why is it so hard to understand that I *want* to be alone?" Sage asked.

"Maybe it is because we don't think that you should be alone right now. Sage, we don't want to see you fall into a downward spiral of self-pity."

She wiped away her tears. "I'm t-tired, Blaze. Please just leave me alone. I'm not about to sink into depression because I broke up with Ryan. I would think that you would know me better than that."

Sage smoothed a lock of hair into place and wiped her face with her hands.

Blaze sat down beside her. "You're right. I'm sorry, sis. It's just that we all know how much you loved this dude."

"I'll get over him," she said. "I just need some time alone right now. I want a couple of days to just grieve the relationship and get myself together. Please give me that," she pleaded.

"Okay." Blaze rose to his feet. "I'll give you two days, and then I'm coming back here to check on you."

Sage watched as Blaze departed, then decided to head to the comfort of her penthouse.

She climbed in bed and stayed there for the rest of the day. Sage had never felt so alone in her life. She knew that her family was only a phone call away, but she could not face them right now. She was too humiliated.

Two days later, Sage emerged from her penthouse looking like a new woman. She knew that everyone would be watching her to make sure she was okay. Sage did not want to dwell any longer on what had happened between her and Ryan. She just wanted to move forward with her life.

It was not going to be easy, however.

Ryan kept popping back into her mind. He had even appeared in her dreams, pleading and asking for another chance. He kept trying to convince her that his motives were pure. Sage did not really care what his motives were now. She just wanted to forget all about Ryan.

Sage prayed she did not run into him. She was not ready to see Ryan and could not handle it right now.

Just as she neared her office, Sage caught sight of Ryan talking with someone from the personnel department. Sage remained rooted in place for nearly ten minutes to avoid him seeing her. She glanced down at her body, struggling to feel something other than despair.

As soon as Ryan walked away, Sage rushed to her office.

She told her assistant that she did not want to be disturbed. Sage sat at her desk behind closed doors, contemplating her future.

Chapter 19

Ryan had not seen Sage in a couple of days, and he was worried about her. He called her but she did not answer her phone. He finally reached out to her mother, who told him that Sage was doing fine but that she wanted some time alone.

He was not ready to give up on Sage. Ryan loved her, and he knew without a doubt that she loved him in return. However, he was not sure they could ever get past his betrayal—Sage had said as much.

He ran into Paige while he was taking a break. "How's the little lady?" he asked.

"Getting bigger every day," she responded. "Cassie's trying to crawl."

"Really?"

Paige nodded with a smile. "My little girl is trying to grow up on me. I'm not sure I'm ready for that. I'm loving this stage of her life so much."

Ryan thought of Sage and his mood changed.

"What's wrong?" Paige inquired. "Did something happen between you and Sage?"

"Things are a little crazy right now, but I'm hoping we will be able to work through it."

"You will," she told him. "You and Sage love each other. It's going to all work itself out."

"I have something I need to tell you," Ryan stated. "I was never really homeless. I only pretended to be so that I could gather material for my article. I'm an investigative reporter."

"I'm not surprised," Paige responded. "I knew there was more to your story than you were telling me. You were too different."

Ryan made a mental note to avoid any personal relationships when working undercover in the future. The mistake could be costly.

"Why all of the secrecy?"

"I write under a pseudonym, and until now it's been kept under wraps."

"You don't have to tell me—"

"I trust you'll keep my secret, Paige," Ryan interjected. "I write as R. G. McCall. Sage found out before I had a chance to tell her myself. She feels betrayed, and she's very upset with me."

"I guess I can see her point," Paige acknowledged.

"I was wrong," Ryan stated. "I know that, but I don't want to lose the one woman I love more than my own life. Paige, I can't lose her. I can't lose Sage."

"I don't think that you will. She loves you just as much as you love her."

Ryan had thought so, too. Now he was not so sure.

* * *

Sage was surprised to see Zaire waiting in her office when she returned from her meeting.

"What are you doing here?"

"I came to check on my big sister," Zaire responded.

"I'm fine," Sage assured her. "It's been hard, but I try to stay busy so that I don't think about him so much."

"Sis, I think you're making a huge mistake."

Sage eyed her sister. "You're supposed to be on my side, Zaire. I was the one betrayed and lied to by Ryan. It was not the other way around."

"I'm on your side, but right is right. Ryan messed up, but this is not something that should keep you two apart like this. He told you that he was going to tell you everything that night. Harold just got the jump on him. Can't you see that you're giving Harold exactly what he wants?"

"I don't care about Harold. Ryan had months to tell me the truth. I'm sorry, but I'm not going to let him off the hook like that. He had multiple opportunities. It only took Harold that one time. Yeah, I know that he set out to cause problems between me and Ryan. He wouldn't have been able to do that if Ryan had just been honest."

"I agree with you to a point," Zaire stated. "Ryan did what he thought was best at the time. However, his intention was to tell you the truth that night."

Sage looked at her sister. "You think I should give him brownie points for that?"

"I think you should consider that you love this man beyond reason. Are you sure that you want to walk away from him?"

"I believed in Ryan," Sage said in a low voice. "I

trusted him. I kept telling Ari and Blaze to give him a chance. I told them how honest and trustworthy he was. All the while, Ryan was plotting behind our backs. He was gathering material to write about our family. He could have asked our permission."

Zaire nodded in understanding. "What is your gut telling you to do?"

Sage was not about to tell her sister how much she wanted to see Ryan or how much she missed him. Her gut kept telling her to go to him, but Sage refused to listen this time around.

"Sis," Zaire prompted.

"I won't ever be able to trust Ryan," she said. "There will always be a question in the back of my mind where he is concerned. I don't want to live that way, and he doesn't deserve to live that way either. It's best that we just go our separate paths."

Zaire rose to her feet. "I guess I would believe it more if you weren't such a bad liar, Sage. I know you, and while you may not want to admit it, you and Ryan belong together and you would be a fool to push him out of your life. He is your soul mate, sis. You won't be whole without him."

Sage opened her mouth to respond, but no words came out.

Zaire gave her a hug. "Just think about what I've said. Don't make this about your ego, Sage. Finding true love is rare. You found it with Ryan, so don't just throw it away. If you're not busy, come out to the house. We can just hang out and watch movies."

Sage smiled. "I'll do that. I'll see you later tonight."

When her sister left, Sage silently considered everything Zaire had said. It was true that she was still madly in love with Ryan, but it bothered her that he had failed to mention he was married before and that he was a reporter. She had let a member of the media into her inner circle. This was something that could lead to disastrous results.

What if he had been some sleazy tabloid reporter?

Sage cringed at the thought. She had not only brought him around her family, but she had shared the most intimate parts of her being.

She left her office a few minutes later.

Meredith was in the hallway. She walked up to Sage and whispered, "I was just coming to see you. I made a reservation at the spa for us. Today is a good day for some pampering."

Sage agreed.

She needed a distraction to take her mind off her heartache.

Ryan packed up the last of his stuff.

A new manager had been hired for Le Magnifique. Sage was still avoiding him, so there really wasn't any reason for him to stay in California any longer. His home was in New York, and he had been gone long enough.

His heart was heavy at the thought of leaving Sage behind.

Ryan glanced around the room, making sure he had everything. He sat down at the desk long enough to write out a check. He had saved all of the money earned from working at the restaurant and planned to donate it to a homeless shelter.

When he finished, Ryan went down to see Paige.

"I just wanted to let you know that I'm going back to New York. I will be on a flight leaving this evening."

"Ryan, can't you work from here?" Paige asked with her eyes full of water. "Do you really have to move back to New York?"

"There's no reason for me to stay here any longer."

"You're wrong," Paige told him. "I'm here and so is Cassie. Sage is here, and if you love her as much as you say that you do, then you'll stay here and fight for her. Ryan, I looked you up on the internet and I've read some of your work. Fight for the woman you love just like you fight for the rights of people in general."

"I have always chosen my battles wisely," he responded. "Sage doesn't trust me anymore, and she doesn't want the relationship."

"She may say that now, but it's going to change."

"I don't think so, Paige. I can't blame her, though. I messed up."

"You shouldn't have to pay for a mistake for the rest of your life."

"Try not to be too hard on Sage. She is in a lot of pain right now. I was the one who messed things up between us."

"I think she's wrong for the way that she's treating you," Paige stated.

"I need you to do me a favor."

"Sure," she responded. "What do you need?"

"I know that you're volunteering at the shelter this weekend. Can you give them this check for me, please? I'm donating all of my earnings from the restaurant to them."

"Oh, my goodness," she murmured. "Sage is crazy if she doesn't realize that you're the real deal."

Sage felt so much better after spending a couple of hours at the spa. She was now ready to go into the office.

"Meredith, thanks so much for scheduling our spa date," Sage said as they stepped off the elevator. "I really needed this."

"Sage, can we talk for a minute?" Meredith inquired as she followed Sage into her office.

"Sure." Sage knew that they were about to discuss Harold's part in her breakup with Ryan.

"I know that Harold had something to do with what happened between you and Ryan. I'm so sorry."

Sage reached over and gave Meredith's hand a squeeze. "It's certainly not anything you have to apologize for. This is all your brother's fault. He will get his—I promise you. Harold will definitely get what is coming to him."

"He wasn't always like this," Meredith said. "He used to be a good brother, friend and confidant."

"For whatever reason, he hates us. Harold is not going to stop messing with us until we stop him. Meredith, we *are* going to put an end to his antics."

"Let me know what I can do to help," Meredith said with a smile.

Meredith left a few minutes later to show one of the units to a prospective buyer.

Sage was stunned when Paige burst into her office saying, "I need to talk to you."

"Paige, is something wrong?" she asked. "Has something happened to Cassie?"

"This has nothing to do with Cassie," she responded. "I just left Ryan."

Sage folded her arms across her chest. "Then I'm sure he must have told you what happened between us."

Paige nodded. "I hope you won't take this the wrong way, but I think you made a huge mistake when you let him leave town."

Sage gasped in surprise. "Ryan's leaving Los Angeles?"

It was Paige's turn to be surprised. "I thought you knew."

"I didn't. Is he moving back to New York?" Sage asked.

"Yes," Paige answered. "He would have stayed here, but Ryan felt that he didn't have a reason to stay. All he needed was one word from you."

"I had no idea that he was leaving," Sage responded. "Ryan and I haven't really talked in the past couple of weeks."

"I know that it's not really my business, but there's something I have to say," Paige began. "Ryan knows that he let things go too far when he kept his identity a secret. He—"

Sage cut her off by asking, "Did you know about this?"

Paige shook her head no. "I just found out this morning when I met with him."

"I know how much Ryan means to you, Paige. I'm not really sure you can be unbiased in this situation. Besides, it really isn't any of your business."

"You're right. It isn't my business, but Ryan confided

in me because he's hurting. Sage, you only had to look at the expression on his face. He is heartbroken."

"I don't think you know him as well as you think you do," Sage pointed out. "After all, you didn't know the truth either, and he considered you a friend."

"I knew from the very first moment I met him that Ryan was a good man. My feelings haven't changed, especially after what happened this morning."

Sage frowned. "What are you talking about?"

"The day you gave Ryan the hundred-dollar bill. That's the day I met him. Cassie was crying, and I didn't have any more diapers, my breast milk was drying up and I had no money. Ryan gave that money to me."

Sage's eyes widened in surprise, but she remained quiet.

"He then bought me lunch and got me a motel room for a month. When I questioned him about the money he was spending, he led me to believe that you had given him a bundle of money. Ryan hadn't known me more than an hour when he did this."

"Okay, so we know that he was a very generous man who cared enough to help out a young mother and her child."

"This morning he gave me this," Paige said, placing the check on Sage's desk. "It's all of the money he earned working here in the restaurant. As you can see, he's donating it to a homeless shelter. So we know something else about Ryan. He puts his money where his mouth is. Wouldn't you agree?"

Sage was too stunned to say anything.

"I know one more thing about Ryan," Paige stated. "He truly loves you."

She picked up the check. "I promised Ryan that I would take this to the shelter."

"Paige…"

She turned around. "Yes."

"Ryan has a good friend in you," Sage stated. "I hope that he will remember how loyal you are to him."

"He has been a great friend to me. He saved my life and my daughter's life, as well. I really hope that you two can work things out. I can see how much you love him."

Sage checked the clock on her desk. "It's almost time for your shift."

"Thank you for hearing me out," Paige stated, "and for not firing me."

"I wouldn't terminate your employment over something like this," Sage assured her. "The truth is that you've given me much to think about."

Paige smiled. "I'm glad to hear it."

Alone in her office, Sage replayed the conversation in her head. Even now after everything that had happened, Ryan continued to surprise her. What he had done for Paige was a wonderful display of love for a fellow human being.

Ryan often talked about paying good deeds forward, and he lived it on a daily basis. She knew that many times he ordered dinners and took them out to the homeless who lingered near the hotel property.

I still feel like he betrayed me. He was supposed to love me enough to be honest. I understand why he kept up the pretense in the beginning, but that should have changed when we began dating.

It was obvious that he had a good heart. Ryan had shown this by his actions. But was it enough to just forgive him? Sage wasn't perfect, but she was not a liar. She never liked playing with others' feelings or deceiving them in any way. She also did not like being on the receiving end either.

This reminded Sage of a time when she was younger. She had been in love with this guy in college. Sage had thought that he returned her feelings until the day he came to her wanting money. He knew her parents owned a couple of hotels and assumed that they were rich. When she refused to ask her parents for five thousand dollars, he turned on her, spouting how he never loved her. He confessed to getting close to her so that he could get money from her. Sage had loaned him a hundred here and there, but after he never paid her back, she stopped giving him money.

He then tried to play on her emotions by telling her that he owed some gangster the five grand because he had a gambling habit. She was later told by a close friend that he had been bragging that Sage was going to give him the down payment for his dream car, a BMW 325i.

That experience left a bad taste in her mouth. From that moment going forward, Sage had zero tolerance for people who pretended to be someone other than themselves.

"Knock, knock…"

Looking up from her computer monitor, Sage drew her attention to the door. "Hey, you…"

Zaire entered the office, saying, "I was in the area, so I figured I'd come by to see if my sister wanted to have lunch with me. I figured we could eat something quick and then do a little shopping."

Sage forced a smile. "I'm really not in the mood for shopping."

Zaire studied her for a moment and then asked, "Did something else happen between you and Ryan?"

"Not really," she responded. "He's moved back to New York. He left yesterday."

"Meaning?" Zaire sat down in one of the visitor chairs facing Sage.

"He's decided to move back home." Sage gave a slight shrug. "It's not like Ryan ever intended to stay in California. He only came out here to gather research on the family."

"I know that was his initial reason, but I'm sure things changed once he met you, sis," Zaire argued. "I actually think that it's perfect because it shows that a woman like you can love a man with nothing to give outside of his heart."

"He played me, Zaire. How do I get past that? Better question is how would you feel if this had happened to you? Would you really be so understanding?"

"No, I'm sure that I would be angry in the beginning. I don't like being deceived any more than you do, but I hope that I wouldn't have tunnel vision in this situation. You have every right to be angry, but at some point you need to move past the anger." Zaire shifted in her seat. "Yes, Ryan should have told you the truth earlier in the relationship, but he can't go back and change the past."

"Zaire, I want to believe in Ryan, but I can't understand why his work was so important to him that he would risk hurting me? Our family is just as normal as everybody else. Why are people so interested in trying to find dirt on us?"

"I don't think he was looking for dirty secrets, Sage. I've read some of his work, and I think he just wanted to contrast or compare us against Robert DePaul's legacy. He's not the type of writer who scours the earth looking for scandals. Ryan is an investigative reporter."

"To be honest, I'm not sure I see the difference between the two." Sage met her sister's gaze straight on. "I don't appreciate anyone spying on our family or using us in his or her articles."

"Why don't you reserve judgment until you read Ryan's article?"

Sage did not respond.

"Sis, give Ryan some credit," Zaire stated. "I know that you do not believe Ryan is going to try and humiliate us in his article."

She sighed in resignation. "I just wish he had been honest with me."

"If you love Ryan as much as I believe you do, then you need to call this man," Zaire advised. "Talk to him."

"You really think I should call Ryan?"

"Yes, I do. Maybe if you had, he would not be in New York right now."

Chapter 20

Sage stared at the telephone. She had been home for about an hour debating whether to call Ryan. What more could be said at this point? They had already gone round and round on the subject.

However, Sage began to wonder if she had given him a fair chance. She had been so angry in the beginning, but now the anger had dissipated. She still felt the sting of his betrayal, and the heartache was still with her at all times.

I miss hearing his voice.

Sage picked up her phone and punched in Ryan's number. She had gotten it from Paige earlier.

Ryan answered on the second ring.

"Hey, it's me."

"Sage, it's good to hear your voice."

"Paige told me that you decided to head back to New

York. I would have said goodbye, but by the time she told me you were already gone."

"I would have told you I was leaving, but you weren't taking my phone calls," he explained. "This was not the way I wanted to leave."

"I understand," she said.

"I love you, Sage," Ryan stated. "You have to know that I would never do anything to hurt you or your family. I had hoped that my reputation as a writer would speak for itself."

"Oh, it does," she responded. "Some of your articles have been very biased to your point of view rather than objective. For example, the article you wrote on women turning thirty and how desperate they are to find a husband."

Ryan released a small chuckle. "That's not an accurate summary of my article, Sage."

"I think it sums it up perfectly," she countered. "Regardless, what you did to me and my family was wrong. My brothers thought I was crazy when they found out we were dating, and I defended you to them. I assured them that your intentions were nothing but honorable. Now I look like a fool."

"I have no problem talking to your brothers and explaining my position. In fact, Blaze and I already had a talk."

"Ryan, this is not the point," Sage interjected. "I fell in love with you. I thought I knew you—the real you. Everything about you seemed real, even when I thought you were homeless. I was wrong."

"We can get past this, sweetheart," Ryan assured her.

"I love you, and I want to spend the rest of my life with you."

Sage didn't respond.

"Did you hear me?" Ryan prompted. "I'm saying that I want to marry you. I know this is not the way a proposal is done. It's certainly not romantic, but it is the truth. I want all of eternity to love you and make up for the pain I caused."

Tears filled Sage's eyes and spilled down her cheeks. "Ryan, I can't think about marriage right now, especially after all that's happened between us."

"Is it because you are worried about what your family will think?" Ryan asked. "Sage, you are a grown woman, and it's time for you to make up your own mind. I know you are loyal to your parents and your siblings, but this is not about them. It's about our loving one another and wanting to be together."

Sage couldn't believe that he would try and make this about her family. "My decision has nothing to do with my family, Ryan," she replied tersely. "I'm not so desperate for marriage that I'd just fall for the first proposal from a man that I'm not sure I can ever trust."

"You are just going to give up on us?"

"There really wasn't an *us*, Ryan," she responded. "It was a facade."

Ryan pulled the tiny box out of the inside pocket of his jacket. He had been filled with hope when she called, but now he was filled with a feeling of hopelessness.

I've lost her.

Ryan felt like kicking himself. He had not meant to upset Sage by proposing.

Talk about bad timing....

He called her back.

"Sage, I'm sorry if I upset you," Ryan said as soon as she answered the phone. "It was not my intent."

"Apology accepted."

"I care about you, Sage. Please don't forget that."

"I know that you do," she said in a small voice. "I still care about you, too, but what we had is over now."

"I guess I have no choice but to accept your decision, Sage. I really miss you. You were the best thing to happen to me. I am a jerk."

"I wouldn't say that exactly," Sage stated. "You are not a jerk."

He wanted to plead for another chance but did not want to upset her any more than he already had. "Sage, I...I wish you well. I hope you will find that special someone who will be all those things you thought you saw in me."

"I can't really think about that right now," she told him.

Ryan loved Sage with all of his heart, and it was tearing him apart to think that after this phone call she would fade from his life forever.

Meredith and Paige showed up at the penthouse to check on Sage at Ryan's request.

"I don't know why he bothered either one of you. I will be okay."

"Honey, I just don't think you should give up like this," Meredith advised. "You and Ryan love each other. I think you should hop on a plane and go to him or ask him to come back here."

Paige agreed.

Sage turned around to gaze at Meredith. "What would you do if you were in my shoes? Could you really forgive so easily?"

"I wouldn't give up so easily on true love," Meredith responded. "I'd keep fighting until there was nothing left to fight for."

"It's too late for me and Ryan," Sage announced. "Our relationship is much too fragile to even consider a long-distance romance. It's best that we move ahead separately."

Paige released a soft sigh. "I'm really sorry to hear that. I was pulling for you and Ryan to get back together."

"Maybe if he were still out here," Sage said, "then we could just take it one day at a time, but he's on the East Coast. It just won't work out."

Sage walked over to one of the huge windows in her penthouse. She stared outside, fighting back tears. Now that Ryan was in New York, there did not seem to be any chance of them ever getting back together.

She thought about his proposal of marriage. The timing was not right to even consider marrying Ryan. Sage had heard the pain in his voice. He really did love her. She was sure of his feelings for her, but what about trust?

Without trust, love did not matter.

Sage opened the large envelope that contained an advance copy of Ryan's article. According to the enclosed note, he had sent one to every member of her family.

She missed him terribly. The past two months had been hard on Sage. She worked long hours and traveled on company business, trying to keep her mind off Ryan. Nothing worked for her.

Ryan haunted her thoughts day and night.

She still loved him, although she kept trying to fight her feelings. She had a couple of guys ask her out, but Sage wasn't ready to embark on another relationship. She needed time to get over Ryan. However, she was not sure she would ever stop loving him.

Sage placed the article on her desk. She wasn't yet ready to read the series that had caused her so much pain.

"Why did you send this to me?" she whispered. "I'm doing everything in my power to get over you."

Her telephone rang.

She smiled when her father's number came up on the caller ID. Picking up, she said, "Hey, Daddy."

"Hey, sugar," Malcolm responded. "Did you receive an advance copy of Ryan's article?"

"I did," she confirmed.

"Have you read it?"

"Not yet. Why?"

"I think you should read it when you have a moment," Malcolm uttered. "I'd like to hear your thoughts when you're done."

Sage was curious. "Sure. I'll sit down and read it shortly."

She ended the call.

"Okay, let's see why my father wants me to read this article," Sage whispered.

*** *

Some 74,000 people live on the streets or in shelters, making the county America's capital of homelessness. They are an incongruous sight amid the shows of superfluous wealth, underscoring the pervasiveness of the huge homeless population in Los Angeles County. They live in parks, bus shelters and alleyways. However, being homeless in this upper-crust enclave is not exactly the same as living on the street in other places.

In this manicured community of 35,000, Rolls-Royces and Lamborghinis glide around the city streets of Beverly Hills, movie stars live in gated mansions and Rodeo Drive price tags provoke gasps from tourists.

"This is the finest place you can be," said Elijah, an affable 59-year-old with a wide grin and a smooth baritone voice who has been homeless in Beverly Hills since 1992.

Sage continued reading. Ryan had done a thorough job in acquiring research for his article.

My experience as a homeless person in Beverly Hills was nothing I expected. I was on the street for one day when I came across an angel. This young woman handed me a hundred-dollar bill, but most importantly, she looked at me as if I were her equal—something most homeless people crave but rarely receive. The next day, "my angel" changed my life completely by offering me a place to stay, clean clothes and employment.

Our generosity is often born out of tragedy; however, generosity is a way of life for the angel and her family, as well. The young woman who came to my rescue is none other than Sage Alexander.

She rescued me because she saw someone who was looking for a second chance—someone who needed a helping hand. Ms. Alexander was there for me, in the same way that Robert DePaul had been there for Franklin, who was homeless at the time.

"There are those people who have a sympathetic thing for us, and we're grateful for it," said a man with grizzled hair pulling a train of wheeled suitcases, an office chair and a stroller piled high with a motley bunch of items found in the trash. He would only identify himself as "Bond."

George, a lanky man who pedals a bicycle around town and sleeps on a building roof, said paparazzi and parking valets can be a problem when he panhandles outside celebrity haunts. However, being close to wealth can lead to one-hundred-dollar handouts or finds such as gold jewelry, video cameras and an Armani suit....

Sage was pleased with the way in which Ryan wrote about her family. It was actually a good article.

She considered calling Ryan but did not. Her heart still belonged to him, and it was just too painful to hear his voice.

"I miss you so much," she whispered.

The article left Sage with mixed emotions. Ryan had done a wonderful job in capturing her family in addition to highlighting the plight of the homeless.

He had proven one important fact: he could be trusted when it came to her family.

Chapter 21

Ryan had hoped to hear from Sage regarding the article once she read it. He had worked hard on the piece and was proud of the way it turned out.

He had hoped that Sage would understand that he never intended to hurt her family, he was seeking the truth.

In a moment of weakness, Ryan considered calling Sage. She dominated his thoughts most of the time. He had tried calling her several times in the past, but she had not responded to any of his calls or emails since that last conversation, so Ryan knew what his heart could not accept: they were over.

Paige Skyped him.

His computer made an audible sound, a notification that Paige was online via Skype. "What's going on?"

"I read the article," she said with a smile. "It's great!"

"Thanks," he murmured.

"Did you send a copy to Sage?" she asked. "I know she'll enjoy reading it."

"I sent her a copy, but I haven't heard anything from her. Hopefully she will get a chance to read it. I want to ease her mind."

"You still love her, don't you?"

Ryan nodded. "I don't think I'll ever love anybody the way that I love Sage."

"So what are you waiting on, Ryan?" Paige asked him. "I know that you are not going to just sit back and let her walk out of your life like that."

"Paige, I love her, but maybe Sage is right. Maybe we don't have a future together."

"You won't have one if you don't talk to her and get this straightened out—that's for sure."

"That's just it, Paige. We can't seem to resolve this."

"That's because you really haven't tried, Ryan," she countered. "Love is worth fighting for. I know that you love Sage, and I know that she loves you just as much. How can you just walk away?"

"Paige, I'm sure you know that it's not what I want at all. I thought Sage and I were trying to build a life together, but apparently I missed something."

"Then don't give up without a fight."

"It's too late, Paige," Ryan told her. "I appreciate that you care about me, but right now I need you to support my decision. Sage left me, and that is the end of it. I need to move on."

"Sure," Paige responded. "I'm sorry if I came off as insensitive."

"You didn't," he assured her. "C'mon, let's talk about something else. Where is my girl?"

"She's right here." Paige lifted the baby so that Ryan could see her.

Ryan smiled at the baby girl and waved. Although temporary, Cassie provided the perfect distraction.

"I'm sure all of you read the advance copy of Ryan's article," Sage announced when she entered the conference room where members of her family had all gathered. "I think he did a great job with it, but I have to apologize for letting him get so close to us. I was careless, and thankfully, my error in judgment did not cause us any embarrassment."

"Do you really believe that you were so wrong about Ryan?" Barbara asked.

"I do," Ari interjected. "She walked what could have been the enemy straight into our camp."

"I disagree," Kellen and Blaze said in unison.

"Sage is a good judge of character," Kellen stated. "She saw the good in this man."

Ari shook his head. "He lied to her about his identity."

"Not really," Natasha countered. "Ryan is who he says he is. He just neglected to mention that he had another persona." She gave Sage a warm smile. "I think you're being too hard on yourself."

"So do I," Blaze contributed. "Sis, I know that you care for Ryan a great deal. Is this really worth giving him up?"

"Look what he did," she responded.

"Sugar, Ryan was accurate in his portrayal of our family," Barbara commented. "I thought it was a wonderful article."

"You all are okay with this?" Sage wanted to know.

"I'm not," Ari answered quickly. "I don't like the way he maneuvered his way into our lives. Deception is just that—deception."

"Honey, I don't agree with you," Natasha told him. "There was no malicious intent on Ryan's part. However, Harold is another story. He wanted to find a way to upset this family, and the only way to do that was to expose Ryan before he had a chance to tell Sage everything. Why are you so willing to ignore that fact?"

Ari considered the words of his wife. After a moment, he uttered, "I had forgotten about Harold's part in all this."

"I still hold Ryan responsible," Sage responded, "but after reading the article, I clearly understand why he pretended to be homeless. It was the best way to experience that way of living."

"The reason I wanted to meet with everyone," Malcolm was saying, "was that Ryan's article was a call to action, in my opinion."

Sage glanced over at Ari. She had no idea where her father was going with this conversation. He seemed excited about something.

"I think that we should continue Robert's legacy by building a homeless shelter. There are not enough shelters in this area. Violence is rising amongst the homeless. Building a shelter will provide more beds and food."

"That's a great idea, Dad," Ari interjected, "but I think if we're going to take on a project like this that we need to make it state-of-the-art."

"In what way?" Sage inquired.

"Ryan mentioned in his article that there are a lot

of people on the streets because of unemployment, for example. Why not provide training for them? Or financial classes?"

"I like your suggestion," Sage said with a smile. "It's a good idea."

Malcolm went around the table, getting everyone's opinion on the project. He smiled when it appeared they agreed.

The first thought in Sage's mind was that Ryan would be thrilled to hear news like this. She could tell from the tone of his writing that he really had a heart for the homeless—not to mention donating his salary to a homeless shelter.

He called her an angel, but Sage had a feeling that he had probably rescued many but kept it a secret. She would never have known about his donation if Paige had not told her. She admired his dedication and had a newfound respect for Ryan's efforts.

"Looks like you are having second thoughts," Kellen said in a low whisper after their meeting.

"I have a much better understanding of the type of man that Ryan is. As it turns out, my gut instincts were right."

"So what are you going to do about it?"

"There's nothing I can do, Kellen," she responded. "I blew it."

Kellen shook his head no. "I don't think so. I'm going to New York to visit some friends. Why don't you come with me?"

Sage frowned. "And do what?"

"Talk to Ryan face-to-face. At this point, it has to be in person."

She had to agree. This was not a conversation Sage could have over a telephone. "I really have to think about this, Kellen. Ryan may have moved on already."

"Sis, if you want your man back, then you need to be swift about it."

Malcolm strolled back into the conference room. "I hadn't realized that you two were in here."

"I was telling Sage that I think she should go to New York to see Ryan face-to-face."

Her father surprised her by agreeing. "I don't need the plane until next week."

"You really think that I should go?" she asked.

Malcolm nodded.

When her father left, Sage glanced over at her brother. "I'm going to New York to see Ryan." She displayed an outward calm that she did not feel. Regardless of what happened after she and Ryan had a chance to talk, Sage owed him an apology. She planned to deliver.

At home, Sage packed for her upcoming trip to New York. She sent up a silent prayer that Ryan would be able to forgive her actions.

"Kellen, I can't do this," Sage uttered when the plane landed. "Coming to New York was a mistake."

"Why do you say that?"

"I can't face Ryan after the way I treated him," Sage told him. "He has probably moved on with his life. I don't want to knock on his door and he's there with some woman."

"Then call him to come to you," Kellen suggested. "Have him meet you for dinner."

"I could probably do that."

"Then what are you waiting for, Sage?"

"What if he doesn't want to see me?" she asked.

"Then you'll have your answer."

Sage stared at her phone for a few minutes, debating whether to make the phone call. She really wanted to see Ryan's handsome face once again. Her heart raced at the mere thought of being in the same room with him.

"So what are you going to do?" Kellen asked.

When Ryan answered his phone, he was shocked to hear Sage's voice on the other end.

"How are you?" he asked.

"I'm fine," she responded softly. "Ryan, I'm here in New York and I...I... Would you like to have dinner with me?"

"When did you have in mind?"

"Tonight."

"I'll see you tonight," he responded. "Just tell me when to be there and where."

"I thought maybe you could handle that little detail," she said. "I don't know much about New York."

"Sage, where are you?"

"I'm on the plane."

"What brings you here to New York?" he asked. Ryan still couldn't believe that Sage was on the other end of the telephone.

"You. I came here to try to speak with you face-to-face. I'm sorry I waited so long to do this."

"You have nothing to be sorry about, Sage."

"I look forward to seeing you, Ryan."

"Same here," he said in response. "I've really missed you, Sage. Write down my address. Hail a cab and have them bring you here. I'll whip up something quick for us to eat."

"Sounds good."

Sage was in New York, and she was on her way to see him. Ryan felt a surge of hope wash over him. He had missed everything about Sage. He still wanted a life with her, and if given the chance, Ryan was going to make good on his proposal.

Ryan could not believe his eyes when he opened the front door. "Sage…" There was so much that he wanted to say, but he could not find the words. His eyes stared lovingly at Sage, drinking in her beauty.

"Can I come in?" she asked softly.

"Yes, of course." Ryan stepped off to the side to allow her entrance. He closed the door behind her.

They stood for a moment just staring at each other.

Ryan reached out, pulling her into his arms. "I have missed you so much."

"I missed you, too."

His lips covered hers.

Sage matched him kiss for kiss.

He picked her up and carried her over to the sofa.

Ryan removed her clothes and then his own.

Fueled by longing and their passion, they made love.

Afterward as they lay snuggled together, Sage said, "Ryan, after I read your article, everything became so clear to me. I understand why you went undercover and why you couldn't tell me. I still wish you could have been honest with me because I never would've told any-one, but I do understand."

"I should have told you about Sandra and the fact that

I had been married before. If our roles were reversed, I would have wanted to know."

Sage kissed him. "I appreciate how you dealt with the article. You did a fabulous job in your depiction of the homeless. You could only have done that by actually walking in their shoes."

"Thank you. When I didn't hear from you…I figured I'd lost you forever."

"I was foolish. I see that now," she said. "Ryan, I'm so sorry for what I put you through. I hope that you can forgive me."

He smiled. "All is forgiven."

"Same here."

Their gaze met and held.

Ryan pulled her back into his arms. "I promise to always be honest with you, Sage. About everything."

Ryan inhaled deeply, sucking in the light floral scent of her perfume. "I've missed you so much."

"Same here," Sage murmured.

"It's time we made some decisions about our relationship and where we're going with it," Ryan blurted.

Sage nodded. "I agree." She wrapped the throw around her body as she sat up. "Can I shower first?"

They showered together.

After getting dressed, they went back into his living room and sat down.

Ryan spoke first. "I love you with my whole heart, but I have to know that we are on the same page."

She nodded. "We are. I made some rash judgments about you, and I won't do that again. I love you so much, Ryan, and I want to be with you."

He smiled. "I love you, too, Sage. Sweetheart, I never stopped loving you."

Desire ignited in the pit of Ryan's belly when he kissed her, the flames growing. Ryan struggled to fight the urge to make love to her again.

"We work, honey," she whispered. "I'm willing to take the risk if you are."

Ryan nodded. "I've been waiting for you to say those very words for weeks. I was about to give up, but then you called."

"Perfect timing," she said with a smile. "I want you, Ryan, and everything that comes with you. We never lost our love for each other. The way we made love proves that. I want a second chance to prove just how much I love you."

"I believe you," he said, smiling.

Sage met his gaze. "Ryan, I can't see my life without you in it. These past few weeks have been so miserable."

Pulling her closer to him, Ryan's lips covered hers, kissing her hungrily. "I'm so glad to have you back, sweetheart," he whispered. "This time I'm not ever letting you go."

"Is that a promise?" Sage asked.

"Yes," he responded. "And I'd like to seal it with this."

Ryan picked up a tiny box and opened it. "I know that we are just getting back together, but I want to start out with you wearing my ring. Sage, will you marry me?"

Tears filled her eyes. "Yes. Yes, I'll marry you."

Chapter 22

One year later

Sage had chosen spring wedding colors in soft shades of purple lilacs, yellow forsythia and accents of green. Ryan had given her total control over the wedding planning, so she enlisted the aid of her mother, Natasha and a wedding planner to create her dream wedding. She glanced down at her engagement ring and smiled.

"If you want the band that goes with that ring, you should start getting ready for your wedding," her sister said from the doorway.

"I can't believe I'm getting married in a few hours, Zaire. This seems like a dream."

"Your wedding is in an *hour*, Sage. Time's flying by."

"I need to get ready."

Zaire chuckled. "Yes, you do. C'mon, Natasha's ready to do your makeup."

Sage followed her sister into the dressing room of the Trinity Christian Church on Catalina Island.

She and Ryan decided that the church on the island provided the perfect setting for their wedding. Rows of seating were garnished with riots of purple lilacs and yellow roses arranged with silver ribbons and baby's breath.

Bridesmaids were adorned in green taffeta gowns with deep V-necks and ruched waistbands, and carried bouquets of flowers bursting in colors of yellow and purple as they floated down the aisle escorted by handsome groomsmen dressed in black tuxedos.

Sage's wedding gown featured a fitted V-neck bodice with straps draped with ruched organza. The skirt was a slim fluted A-line skirt with a very full organza overskirt. The low back laced up with organza ties that fell down the back of the gown onto the beautiful flowing chapel-length train.

"You look like an angel," her father said. He was standing in the doorway of the dressing room. "I always thought I'd be prepared for the day when I would have to give you to another man. I thought I'd be ready...."

"Daddy, please don't make me cry."

"You are a precious jewel, daughter. I made sure that we had father-daughter dates so that you would know what to expect from a man. Your mother and I raised you to know your self-worth. Sage, you have made us so proud."

"I love you, Daddy."

Malcolm took her by the hand. "I love you, too, sugar.

Ryan is a good man, and I know that he will take good care of you."

"And I will take good care of him," Sage responded. "We will take our vows today and become one. He will be my life partner and I will be his."

Malcolm smiled. "Your mother told you about the vows we made to one another at our wedding."

Sage nodded. "I'm so ready to be Ryan's wife."

"Then I guess I'd better get you to the altar."

The bridesmaids and groomsmen were in a line and ready to make their entrance. Her mother was about to be escorted to her seat but paused to give Sage one last hug before she became a married woman.

Sage shivered in anticipation as the processional began. In a few seconds, she would be walking down the aisle on the arm of her father. Her whole being seemed to be filled with waiting.

She saw the heartrending tenderness of Ryan's gaze. He looked so handsome in his tuxedo.

Sage broke into a smile when her father placed her hand in Ryan's care. When it was time for them to take their vows, Ryan spoke first.

He looked down into her eyes and said, "Sage, I can't put into words how much I love you. I want you to know that I will forever love and honor you. Our love will prevail through good times and bad. Today, I pledge my heart to you till death do us part."

Ryan's grin grew wider, making Sage's heart skip a beat. "It is my honor to be your husband." His deep baritone voice died off, watered down by his tears.

Sage was too choked up to immediately respond.

Ryan's words had touched her deeply. She knew he had meant every word spoken. She cleared her throat softly and then said, "Ryan, I will forever love and honor you. I love you dearly, and I know that a love like ours will prevail through tough times and good times. You are my life partner and I am yours. I pledge my heart to you till death do us part."

There was more she wanted to say to Ryan, but she was too emotional to find the right words.

The pastor spoke a few words before saying the words Sage and Ryan wanted to hear most. "I now pronounce you man and wife…."

Ryan exhaled a long sigh of pleasure. He pulled Sage into his arms, drawing her close. He pressed his lips to hers, mindful that they were not yet alone. Reluctantly, Ryan settled for a chaste kiss, instead of the lingering, passionate one he desired.

Grinning, Ryan escorted his bride down the aisle and through the double exit doors at the back of the church. They escaped into the dressing room until it was time to go back into the chapel for the wedding photographs.

His eyes traveled down the length of her, nodding in obvious approval. "You look so beautiful, sweetheart."

Sage broke into a big smile. "Ryan, can you believe it? *We're actually married!* You are mine, baby." She glanced down at the four-carat sapphire engagement ring with its matching platinum band on her left hand. "I've dreamed of this day for so long, Ryan."

They were not alone for long. Bridesmaids and groomsmen burst into the room, putting a halt to their unspoken words of love for each other.

Amid congratulatory wishes, Ari pulled Sage off to

the side before they headed back into the sanctuary for pictures. "I'm happy for you, sis. I guess I should never doubt your instincts."

"Thank you for saying that, Ari. I appreciate it."

"You were right, and I was wrong. I can admit it."

Ari cast a look over his shoulder to where Ryan stood talking with his brother. He turned back to face her. "He better be good to you."

"I really don't think you have to worry about that. He's a good man, Ari. He treats me like a queen."

"That's as it should be." Ari glanced over his shoulder once again. Ryan was holding a conversation with their parents.

Sage followed his gaze. "I love him so much."

Natasha joined them. "You two looked like you were having a serious conversation. Is everything okay?"

"I came to congratulate my sister and to tell her that I was wrong about Ryan," Ari stated.

His wife kissed him on the cheek. "I'm so proud of you."

Barbara walked over, saying, "Honey, the photographer's waiting on you and Ryan."

"I love you, Mrs. Manning," Ryan whispered as they posed for pictures.

Sage broke into a smile. "I love you, too, Mr. Manning."

"You have made me the happiest man on this earth, sweetheart. I never thought I could be this happy."

She stared him in the eye and responded, "I feel the same way, Ryan."

He pulled her closer to him. "Thank you for giving

me another chance, Sage. I promise there will be no more secrets between us. In fact, there is something I need to tell you."

"What is it?"

"Keith is going to propose to Paige in just a few minutes."

"Really?"

Ryan nodded. "I hope you don't mind, but when he asked me about it, I thought it was a great idea."

"I don't have a problem with it," Sage assured him. "I actually think it's very romantic."

The pictures taken, Mr. and Mrs. Ryan Manning were delivered in a horse-drawn carriage to the hotel where the reception was being held.

Sage was excited about beginning her new life with Ryan. She felt as if she had been waiting her whole life for him.

The wait was finally over.

Epilogue

Sage and Ryan entered the ballroom where a news conference was about to begin. They joined the rest of her family, who were already there. Even Zaire and Kellen had flown in for the event.

Ryan was very excited about the project they had been working on. The homeless did not get much attention from the media, but that was about to change.

Sage nudged him gently in the arm. "What are you thinking about?"

"What's about to happen," he responded. "We are about to change lives."

She nodded in agreement. "This is all because of you, Ryan. If you hadn't written that article, my father may not have had this idea."

Ryan grinned. "I'm glad I could help."

Sage nudged him slightly harder this time around.

The news conference was about to start, so she and Ryan took their places at the table.

Shortly before he and Sage got married, Ryan had decided to quit living in R. G. McCall's shadow. He publicly acknowledged that he was the investigative reporter and announced that he would no longer be writing under the pseudonym.

Ryan spoke first.

"What is the true face of homelessness? It's not that man you see at the busy intersection, holding the sign, begging for change. He's just familiar, and he's pretty convenient for massaging society's conscience. The face of homelessness is the same as you and me. We want to find solutions, but the fact is that nothing will change until people grasp that a poorly performing public school system, inadequate public transportation, a lack of affordable housing and unemployment have more to do with homelessness than the more ready rationale— someone choosing to live on the street."

Ryan paused a moment before continuing. "Robert DePaul's desire was to find a way to help the homeless, but he knew that it would take more than money. His son, Malcolm Alexander, decided to pick up the torch. My father-in-law will detail our plans to help combat this growing population."

Sage reached under the table and gave his hand a light squeeze.

Malcolm stood up and removed the canvas that covered the model of the Robert DePaul Center.

"What will distinguish this shelter from the others is that we will be offering weekly support meetings for substance abuse, financial counseling and career counseling. The first floor will feature the kitchen, barbershop and four classrooms with computers. The second floor of the three-story building has three dorm areas and rooms lined with bunks that can sleep 600 people...."

The news conference was barely over before news of the newest Los Angeles mission was the subject of tweets circulating around the world. Ari's assistant was already fielding interview requests.

"That Twitter is something else," Barbara commented.

Zaire held up her phone. "They are calling the center the rock star of the homeless shelters."

"They are even tweeting about the à la carte menu," Kellen announced with a chuckle. "This is crazy. Fried chicken, hot dogs... I guess we got it going on."

Sage stood beside Ryan as he talked with a friend of his, who was also a reporter.

"I hope you'll let me have an exclusive when this seventeen million in new construction is ready. I'd like a tour."

"Of course," Ryan promised.

They decided to have lunch at Le Magnifique with the rest of the family. Afterward, they headed up to the penthouse.

"You looked like you missed working in the restaurant," Sage told Ryan. "I saw the way you were checking everything out. You had this look in your eye. You miss Le Magnifique."

"I do," he confessed. "I enjoyed my time there. I've been thinking that I'd like to open another restaurant— in Los Angeles."

"Really?" Ryan continued to travel to New York on business, but he had moved all of his things to Beverly Hills. He and Sage were building a house, as they wanted to put some distance between the business and their personal lives.

Ryan nodded. "How do you feel about it?"

"I think it's a great idea. Honey, you should do it."

"You won't mind?"

"No, not at all," she told him. "In fact, I will help you. I used to be a hostess on the weekends for a restaurant back home when I was in high school."

"Sage, you're incredible."

"That's why you married me, right?" she asked with a grin.

"That's part of it," Ryan stated honestly. "The other is that you were a temptation I could not resist."

Sage laughed before throwing a pillow at him.

* * * * *

REQUEST YOUR FREE BOOKS!

2 FREE NOVELS
PLUS 2 FREE GIFTS!

KIMANI™
ROMANCE

Love's ultimate destination!

YES! Please send me 2 FREE Kimani™ Romance novels and my 2 FREE gifts (gifts are worth about $10). After receiving them, if I don't wish to receive any more books, I can return the shipping statement marked "cancel." If I don't cancel, I will receive 4 brand-new novels every month and be billed just $4.94 per book in the U.S. or $5.49 per book in Canada. That's a saving of at least 21% off the cover price. It's quite a bargain! Shipping and handling is just 50¢ per book in the U.S. and 75¢ per book in Canada.* I understand that accepting the 2 free books and gifts places me under no obligation to buy anything. I can always return a shipment and cancel at any time. Even if I never buy another book, the two free books and gifts are mine to keep forever.

168/368 XDN FEJR

Name	(PLEASE PRINT)	

Address		Apt. #

City	State/Prov.	Zip/Postal Code

Signature (if under 18, a parent or guardian must sign)

Mail to the **Reader Service:**
IN U.S.A.: P.O. Box 1867, Buffalo, NY 14240-1867
IN CANADA: P.O. Box 609, Fort Erie, Ontario L2A 5X3

Not valid for current subscribers to Kimani Romance books.

Want to try two free books from another line?
Call 1-800-873-8635 or visit www.ReaderService.com.